Damn the Torpedoes

Brian Burrell

Damn the Torpedoes

FIGHTING WORDS, RALLYING CRIES, AND THE HIDDEN HISTORY OF WARFARE

McGraw-Hill

New York   San Francisco   Washington, D.C.   Auckland   Bogotá
Caracas   Lisbon   London   Madrid   Mexico City   Milan
Montreal   New Delhi   San Juan   Singapore
Sydney   Tokyo   Toronto

Library of Congress Cataloging-in-Publication Data
Burrell, Brian
    Damn the torpedoes : fighting words, rallying cries, and the
hidden history of warfare / Brian Burrell.
      p. cm.
    Includes bibliographical references (p.).
    ISBN 0-07-134262-1 (alk. paper)
    1. War. 2. Combat. 3. Military art and science. 4. Military
history. I. Title.
    U21.2.B86 1999
    355'.009—dc21   99-21405
                                            CIP

McGraw-Hill

*A Division of The **McGraw·Hill** Companies*

Passages from Leo Tolstoy's *War and Peace* are from the 1922 translation by Louise and Aylmer Maude.

Title page: The maintop of the *Hartford*, with howitzer. From a sketch by Walton Taber for the *Century Magazine*.

1 2 3 4 5 6 7 8 9 0 DOC/DOC 9 0 4 3 2 1 0 9

ISBN 0-07-134262-1

McGraw-Hill books are available at special quantity discounts to use as premiums and sales promotions, or for use in corporate training programs. For more information, please write to the Director of Special Sales, McGraw-Hill, Inc., 11 West 19th Street, New York, NY 10011. Or contact your local bookstore.

 This book is printed on recycled, acid-free paper containing a minimum of 50% recycled, de-inked fiber.

Contents

Nelson at Trafalgar. Engraving from a painting by William H. Overend.

Introduction

At the siege of Malta in 1565, Jean de la Valette, Grand Master of the Knights of Malta, urged his men on with the dramatic words: "Come, my knights, and let us all go and die there! This is the day!" The image is splendid, if not compelling. Surely this is how a great commander leads his troops to brilliant victory or glorious defeat. Or is it? Has anyone ever talked this way on the battlefield?

On closer inspection, Valette's words hardly do justice to the event, whether he actually spoke them or not. There was no day of reckoning. The siege of this small Mediterranean island stronghold lasted from May to September. And it was the Turks who did the besieging, while Valette and his knights mounted a defense; they did not have to "go" anywhere—they were already there. A gritty act of defiance it was, but only the timely arrival of the Spanish fleet forced the Turks to break the siege and go home. In other words, Valette's stirring battle order, selected out of all the things he might have said by way of symbolizing this great struggle, has almost no connection to the event itself. But it sounds good.

We have it on better evidence that on D-Day in 1944, a far less excitable Dwight D. Eisenhower launched the largest invasion in history with the laconic phrase: "Okay, let's go." If nothing else, this is believable. Historians, of course, are understandably loath to set the wheels of history in motion with such unassuming words. In this case they didn't have to. Eisenhower obliged the press and other shapers of posterity with a more formal send-off that better suited the gravity of the moment. "The eyes of the world are upon you," he announced, "the hopes and prayers of liberty-loving people everywhere march with you." That was for the folks back home. For the men who would be doing the fighting, the only words that mattered were: "Okay, let's go."

Any good war story needs dialogue, and historians have a knack for coming up with it whether it was actually spoken or not. They understand that the chaotic nature of the event demands a dramatic framework if those who were not there are to make sense of it. Even those who *were* there need such a framework. After all, the frontline soldier's impressions of a battle are often limited to perhaps a few hundred yards of entrenchments or to a single gun battery. He too needs some larger sense of what it was all about—what was accomplished and what was at stake. This is when the words of a Jean de la Valette or a Dwight D. Eisenhower come in handy. They affirm that as awful as the event itself may have appeared at the time, it was really about glory, about honor, and about principles.

And it is not merely principles that are at stake. The reality of war cries out for euphemisms, if not outright lies. Fear, hesitation, loss of composure, and dereliction of duty all figure into every battle, but have to be covered up if an army is to retain its morale. Some small victory must be found in each defeat; those who died ignominiously must be cited for their heroic sacrifice; acts of indecisiveness or stupidity must be transformed into instances of tactical brilliance; even quietly brilliant leadership has to be spruced up or fitted out with inspired words to meet the demands of the occasion. When it all spews out in the annals of war, it should redound to the glory of arms and the man.

Unfortunately, the result is often history writ too large. When everything that detracts from a stirring narrative is altered or jettisoned, the doctored script often reads like the panels of an action comic book. Every quote from a commander ends in an exclamation point, firefights miraculously fade into silence while sergeants rally their platoons, and the enemy graciously holds off an artillery barrage so that a lieutenant colonel can deliver a homily in the field. While we all know that even quarterbacks sometimes have difficulty making themselves heard by ten other players in a hostile stadium, popular representations of battle would have us believe that a cavalry officer can regale his men with a fine speech in the midst of a cannonade.

Then there are the inevitable clichés. "Crack troops" are "mown down like wheat before a scythe," arrows and bullets "fall like hail," the regiment stands up to a "withering fire" before they are all "slain to a man." Faced with the task of describing events they did not see and cannot imagine, many history writers routinely resort to similarly overworked phrases that have peppered revisionist battle descriptions since the days of Homer.

The result is a highly skewed depiction of battle, stripped bare of any vestige of psychological plausibility or physical possibility. The actions of individual soldiers are subsumed by the movements of platoons, companies, regiments, and battalions. A thousand individual struggles are effaced by capsule summaries of major offensives. The complex task of deploying thousands of soldiers becomes a sweeping arc on a map, a piece slid across a game board. As more and more details fall by the wayside, it is not uncommon for an epic battle to be reduced to nothing more than a few breathless words of exhortation. In the Bible's Book of Judges, we hear Gideon's instructions to his band of 300: "When I blow with a trumpet, I and all that are with me, then blow ye the trumpets on every side of all the camp, and say, 'The sword of the Lord, and of Gideon.'" After which there is little more to say—the Midians are routed out of Israel. With the words "Once more into the breach, dear friends, once more," Shakespeare sums up Henry V's assault on the walls of Harfleur. The Battle of Trafalgar? "Say to the fleet, England expects that every man will do his duty." That was Horatio Nelson. Waterloo? "To every Frenchman who has a heart, the moment has now arrived to conquer or die." That was Napoleon. The Duke of Wellington countered with, "Whatever happens, you and I will do our duty." And then, of course, there is, "Damn the torpedoes! Full speed ahead!"—which stands for something, but what?

This is a book about war viewed through the filtering lens of fighting words and battle cries. It explores the phenomenon of getting troops to charge, getting them to bring fire on the enemy, getting them to retreat, and then getting everyone to agree on what happened. It is not as simple as it may appear. In recounting incidents of glorious defiance and of inglorious surrender, the "truth" usually comes about through a process of consensus in which many details are left behind. This book reveals what standard battle narratives leave out—how real men (rather than two-dimensional heroes) have gone into battle, how they have dealt with fear, and how their stories have been transformed into stale narratives that hide the more interesting realities of war. It is not simply a collection of war stories, but a guide to reading war stories—what motifs to look for and how to tell when facts are being used selectively or not at all. Admittedly, efforts to point out the "truth" in a subject that elicits such strong feelings are not always well received. For many readers, challenging popular history is tantamount to debunking anything that smacks of heroism, duty, or sacrifice. But my objective is not to debunk. It is instead to portray warfare as a believably human activity rather than as an otherworldly exercise.

At first glance the chapter titles read like a grab bag of clichés, but behind each one lie some useful truths and many fascinating tales. "Fire at will," for example, was for Napoleon the only practical method of infantry fire. Yet the phrase also has a subtle irony. The average infantryman of the gunpowder era, it turns out, not only was reluctant to shoot to kill, but more often than not fired harmlessly in the air. Many soldiers were unwilling to shoot at all. This fact, combined with the well-documented inefficiency of small arms fire, sheds new light on the meaning of the all-too-familiar words, "Don't fire until you see the whites of their eyes." What may sound quaint to us now made perfect sense in the context of the weaponry, formations, and battle tactics of eighteenth-century regimental warfare. Far from being one of history's little white lies, the words open a door into an often misunderstood past.

A few of the chapters range a bit far afield. Chapter 7 uses a Shakespearean line as a point of departure for an examination of the misuse of numbers in military history. Chapter 10 is a rumination on another theme—the sharp dividing line between those who have seen battle and those who have not. Finally, because it is presumptuous for any book, especially one on this subject, to claim to have a monopoly on the truth, some suggestions for further reading are provided for those who care to follow up, if not check up, on points made here.

As for the phrase that serves as the title of this book, it stands apart because it is by now so far removed from the occasion that inspired it as to be almost meaningless. But it too has a story, and an instructive one, and so it is a fitting device with which to frame the beginning and end of this inquiry.

The best protection against the enemy's fire is a well-directed fire from our own guns.

Flag Officer David G. Farragut
General order for the passing of the Union fleet
by Port Hudson, Louisiana
13 March 1863

Don't flinch from the fire, boys, there's a hotter fire for those who don't do their duty. Give that rascally tug a shot!

Farragut
At the passing of Fort St. Philip
Battle of New Orleans
24 April 1862

Damn the glasses!

Farragut
To his Signal Officer at Fort St. Philip

1

The passage of the forts below New Orleans, April 24, 1862. From a drawing by J.O. Davidson for Battles and Leaders of the Civil War.

CHAPTER ONE

Don't Flinch from the Fire, Boys!

THE BATTLE OF NEW ORLEANS (1862)

Fighting Words

Over a hundred years ago the expression "Damn the torpedoes!" symbolized one of America's proudest military moments. Most Americans knew not only who said it, but why he said it, what it meant to the course of one battle, and what that battle meant to the nation as a whole. Yet today it survives as little more than a figure of speech. Lumped together with John Paul Jones's "I have not yet begun to fight" and Commodore Perry's "Don't give up the ship," it is often mistaken for a relic from the Revolutionary War, the War of 1812, or even World War II. Few people have any idea what it means. What were these torpedoes, and why damn them?

"Damn the torpedoes," it turns out, belongs to Admiral David Farragut in the way that "To be or not to be" belongs to Hamlet. The expression is quoted so often that the circumstances which inspired it are more or less forgotten. That Farragut said it at the Battle of Mobile Bay on August 5, 1864 is only slightly more revealing than the fact that Hamlet delivers his famous soliloquy in act 3, scene 1. As for what Farragut meant, the question is clouded by the probability that he never said "Damn the torpedoes" at all. The only thing we can be sure of is that he would have preferred to be remembered for something else.

The point here is not to make a long story short. David Farragut was credited with words he probably never said because his actions at Mobile Bay suited the moment and the words suited the actions. Not every crisis leads to such a fortuitous combination, but most inspiring battle orders come about like this. Not actually spoken in the heat of battle, they later emerge to capture the moment in a satisfying way—so satisfying that no one is inclined to deny them later.

As we are occasionally reminded, no event is historical until someone puts it into words. Like most men who have made history, David Farragut was not aware of doing it at the time. It was only after the events themselves, once he had a chance to reflect on the battle and compose his official report, that the mechanism of history was set in motion. But it is a quirky mechanism. Farragut never mentioned having said "Damn the torpedoes" or anything like it, nor did any other participant or onlooker at the time. The official reports of the Battle of Mobile Bay fill hundreds of pages. Contemporary newspaper and magazine writers embellished the record, and poets even weighed in with heroic verse, but none of these chronicles so much as alluded to the famous phrase. It surfaced only years later, when Farragut was no longer around to refute it, and it has managed to outlive both his memory and that of the battle itself.

How this could come about cannot be explained by a mere recitation of events at Mobile Bay. It helps to know something about how Farragut came to be there and how his story came to be told—in short, to consider how war becomes history. To that end we may as well, as Mr. Peabody would say, set the way-back machine to two years before the Battle of Mobile Bay, and discover how it was that David Farragut first came to national prominence.

A Sailor of Fortune

In November of 1861, seven months into the American Civil War, the Secretary of the United States Navy, Gideon Welles, was looking for a naval commander he could trust with an important assignment—capturing the Confederate stronghold at New Orleans. This would be the first step in gaining control of the Mississippi River for the North, thus cutting off the lifeblood of the Confederacy. The task, as Welles saw it, would require "courage, audacity, tact, and fearless energy, with great self-reliance, decisive judgment, and ability to discriminate and act under trying and extraordinary circumstances." The man he had in mind was a 61-year-old captain with over 50 years of naval experience, a man Welles hoped would turn out to be an American Nelson.

David Farragut longed to see action in the Civil War. Distrusted by some Northerners because of his ties to the South (he was born in Virginia and had married a Southerner), he spent the early stages of the war in a frustrating state of limbo, waiting for an assignment that looked as if it would never come. When asked whether he thought New Orleans could be taken and whether he was willing to do it, he jumped at the opportunity and easily convinced Welles that there was no other man for the job. Thus in January of 1862, Farragut found himself in charge of the wooden steam frigate *Hartford*, heading for the Gulf of Mexico to assume command of a flotilla of 17 steam gunboats and 20 mortar schooners. It was the largest war fleet the nation had ever assembled. Of the 4000 sailors who manned it, some would die soon, but those who lived would witness the meteoric rise of a true American hero and would leave behind their testimony to how it all came about.

Easily the most intriguing of the witnesses was B. S. Osbon, identified by some as a correspondent for the *New York Herald*, by others as a signal officer on the *Hartford*, and by still others as the ship's clerk. He was apparently all of these things, a Zelig-like figure whose knack for being at the center of the action marked him as either a man of destiny or one whose story we should approach with caution. Apparently a seasoned hand on board warships, Osbon, by his own account, served as Farragut's factotum in the Mississippi campaign, standing by his flag officer's side during the action, always at the ready to do what was needed in key moments of decision. Forty years later he would dictate his memories to the author Albert Bigelow Paine, a writer known primarily as Mark Twain's first biographer. The resulting chronicle, entitled *A Sailor of Fortune*, describes many colorful and seminal episodes in American history, among them Farragut's campaign to seize control of the lower Mississippi, an event that in itself would make the admiral a famous man. This was not, however, the occasion of Farragut's most famous words. They were "spoken" some 15 months later at Mobile Bay. At that time, for reasons unknown, Osbon was no longer serving under Farragut, and we have to do without the clerk's version of those celebrated events. Still, Osbon's recollections of the New Orleans campaign are vivid enough, and they tell us a few useful things about how legends are born.

Farragut's task at New Orleans is easily described. To reach it he needed to get past two forts that lay on opposite banks of the Mississippi about 30 miles downriver from the city. Confederate forces had made this as difficult as possible by forcing Farragut to choose between two unappealing options. One was to neutralize the forts by bombarding them. The other, which at first seemed too dangerous, was to run the fleet by the guns. The option of doing nothing, a policy that Lincoln's generals had tried too many times, was one that the President would no longer tolerate. Lincoln demanded results, and Farragut had been appointed to get them.

Yet the newly appointed flag officer initially chose the safer and more time-consuming first course, and during eight days of shelling his fleet put on a display whose magnificent spectacle was rivaled only by its astounding ineffectiveness. General Benjamin Butler, whose ground troops came along in support of Farragut's fleet, called the bombardment "superbly useless," a reference to the high percentage of short-fused bombs that burst in the air, resulting in some dazzling fireworks but surprisingly little damage.

Faced with a stalemate that constituted a defeat, Farragut took his first important step toward immortality by switching to the second option, the one that would become his trademark. By running the forts, which is to say, by sailing his fleet under the well-placed guns of enemy fortifications, Farragut risked exposing his men to possible annihilation. All he could do to counter the risk was to keep up a steady barrage of his own and hope that the Confederates would shoot poorly. "The best protection against enemy fire," he assured himself, "is a well-directed fire by our own guns." The stakes were high. The strategy amounted to an all-or-nothing proposition where "all" constituted a crippling blow to the Confederacy, and "nothing" meant less than nothing, not only defeat but shame and scandal for Farragut—an ignominious end to a long naval career.

Farragut, by all accounts, possessed the requisite aplomb for the job, the ability to appear calm and focused while all around him went to pieces. His ship's surgeon, Jonathan Folts, called him a "bold, brave officer, full of fight," yet admitted that the commander "evidently does not know what he is going about." Although an air of indecisiveness plagued Farragut at times, he never cowered before mortal danger, and this did not go unnoticed. Under bombardment during a reconnaissance of the forts, he is said to have marveled at the incoming shells with a schoolboy's delight. "There comes one!" he exclaimed. "There! There! Ah, too short; finely lined though."

Although careless of his own safety, Farragut showed great concern for his men. On the night before executing his plan, he turned to his clerk and asked, "What do you estimate our casualties will be, Mr. Osbon?" Like many fatherly commanders, Farragut dreaded the notion of losing any of his boys, and was surprised when Osbon came back with an estimate of a mere hundred casualties out of a few thousand men. Farragut assumed it would be much worse, but Osbon reasoned as follows: "Well, most of us are pretty low in the water, and, being near, the enemy will shoot high. Then, too, we will be moving and it will be dark, with dense smoke. Another thing, gunners ashore are never as accurate as gunners aboard a vessel." Farragut reflected a bit and said, "I wish I could think so, I wish I could be as sure of it as you are."

At that moment something extraordinary happened. As Farragut paced the deck, lost in thought, Osbon scanned the sky looking for signs of the next day's weather, and was amazed to see a great bald eagle circling the Union fleet. "Look there, Flag Officer," he cried out to Farragut, "that is our national emblem. It is a sign of victory." Although of questionable military use, the bird did seem to be a portent of good things to come. Before a great battle the ancient Greeks routinely looked for such favorable signs in the entrails of sacrificed animals or in the arrangement of the heavens. It was every commander's duty to search out some indication of the gods' favor, and as Osbon makes clear, this idea still held considerable fascination for modern-day warriors.

Or it could simply have been a case of inspired imitation. If Osbon had been paging through the *Annals* of the Roman historian Tacitus, he might have stumbled upon a remarkably similar eve-of-battle scene at the camp of the Roman general Germanicus, whose "attention was arrested by a curiously happy omen—eight eagles [one for each of his eight legions] seen aiming for, and entering, the glades. 'Forward,' he exclaimed, 'and follow the birds of Rome, the guardian spirits of the legions!'" Tacitus, of course, had made the whole thing up.

At one o'clock the next morning Farragut sent Osbon aloft to the mizzen peak of the *Hartford* with two red lanterns, the signal for the weighing of anchors. Within two hours the fleet of warships was underway, moving in single file through river barriers that Farragut's men had breached the day before. The mortar schooners moved into firing range. The moment of crisis had now been reached. With his 50 years' experience at sea behind him, and after months of preparation for the greatest undertaking of his career, Farragut was about to initiate a venture of a few hours' duration that would catapult him to national prominence and make him a hero. Clearly the Union needed heroes, and the attention of the world, it would seem, converged for the moment on this single event.

Of course, this kind of breathless contextualizing is all hindsight, a narrative device better suited to Hollywood than to history books. For Farragut and his men, this moment was part of another day's work. It was an important day to be sure, but the gunners at the forts were the only audience the flag officer and his crew had in mind.

Briefly stated, Farragut needed to get through a Scylla and Charybdis formed by Forts Jackson and St. Philip, two defiant sentinels placed nearly opposite each other at a point where the river was about a third of a mile wide. Fort Jackson, the larger of the forts, held 95 guns; Fort St. Philip had just 52. In addition, a small Confederate fleet lay in wait above the forts, including among its dozen armed vessels an iron-plated tugboat that had been converted into a ram, always a threat to wooden ships. The Union fleet, possessing about 180 guns, would divide its fire between the forts. But because each ship would pass in single file, the fleet's total fire could not be brought simultaneously. Farragut had wanted to proceed in double column, with pairs of ships lashed together. This would have made the column shorter while increasing its concentration of fire. But the narrowness of the breach in the river barrier, along with uncertainty about the width of the navigable channel, forced him to run the ships through in single file, thus exposing each one to fire from both sides. All in all they appeared to be sitting ducks.

Yet when the firing commenced, Osbon's conjectures proved to be largely correct. As in most military engagements, chance and confusion took over. The rising moon illuminated the fleet, but as soon as the batteries began firing the entire theater of action became engulfed in a pall of smoke. The gunners in the forts concentrated their fire on the flashes of the ships' guns, which was all they could see, and their aim was indeed poor.

As the *Hartford* made its approach, Osbon hoisted the Stars and Stripes in defiance not only of standard procedure but of common sense. The crew had spent the previous day painting the ship black and arranging other camouflaging, an effort rendered pointless by the colorful flags flying atop each mast above the smoke. Farragut bellowed at the clerk, demanding to know what the hell he was doing. But Osbon, never at a loss for words, replied: "I thought if we are to go down, it would look well to have our colors flying above the water." Osbon's rationale passed muster, and in a show of reckless bravado often seen in military men on the front lines, the commanders of the other Union ships followed suit. It hardly mattered. The flashes from the ships' guns made for good enough targets. At the same time, their very firepower made the fleet anything but sitting ducks.

Because Farragut was trying to conserve ammunition, he withheld firing from the *Hartford* as long as he could, thus escaping most of the initial barrage. He eventually sent Osbon forward to see if the bow guns would bear upon the fort, and when the clerk relayed a confirmation, the commander gave the order to load and fire at will. Presented with this new target, the Confederate gunners now began to concentrate their fire on the *Hartford*, and as they poured solid shot, grapeshot, and explosive shells onto the fleet, the Northerners gave it right back. Farragut would note later in his report, "It was as if the artillery of heaven were plying upon earth."

Because of the low-hanging smoke, Farragut climbed into the port rigging to get a better view, leaving Osbon to flutter anxiously on deck as bombs exploded, grapeshot rained down, and several crew members were blown to pieces. Knowing that batteries have a tendency to shoot too high, Farragut understood that the rigging was a dangerous place to be, as did Osbon, who recalled climbing partway up and shouting, "We can't afford to lose you, Flag Officer. They'll get you, up here, sure." When this appeal didn't work, the clerk tried a different tack: "Flag Officer, they'll break my opera glasses if you stay up there." Osbon had just lent Farragut a pair of glasses, and thought an appeal for their safety might get more sympathy. But this plea didn't work either. It merely inspired a comeback that seems either too good to be true, or damning evidence of a rhetorical habit that plagued the flag officer and would become his trademark.

"Damn the glasses!" Farragut barked down at Osbon. (Because the ship was already steaming ahead at full speed, there was nothing to add.) But Osbon persisted: "It's you we want. Come down!" At that Farragut relented and climbed down. Almost immediately a shell tore through the rigging where the flag officer had been perched. The intrepid clerk had just preserved a national institution.

Is It to End This Way?

None of the details of this account, aside from those concerning manpower, ship strength, and weaponry, can be known for certain. We can safely claim that Farragut ran his fleet between the batteries of Forts Jackson and St. Philip, that he sustained some losses, that he made it through, overpowered the Confederate ships, and took New Orleans. In some historians' view this effectively ended the possibility of victory for the South. We can safely go on to conclude that the situation at the forts was chaotic, dangerous, stressful, and uncertain. But the human side of it—what it must have been like to the participants, who said what, and who did what (which is the stock in trade of all military history writing)—is largely a matter of speculation, if not outright fabrication.

Osbon, for one, is too literary to be believed. The shell that rips through the rigging just after Farragut has climbed down, the eagle straight out of Roman legend, and the rather far-fetched tale of the opera glasses read like a Hollywood script (making it all the more surprising that this scene has never been reenacted on film). The intrepid clerk also seems

11

to anticipate every eventuality that is properly in the captain's domain. He assesses the battle conditions in order to make an estimate of expected casualties. (He underestimated; they amounted to 37 killed and 149 wounded.) He tries to ascertain the weather that will prevail. He gives the signal to weigh anchor. He even orders his flag officer off the rigging, albeit pleadingly.

Osbon is nothing less than a character out of the pages of fiction, the supercompetent assistant bound by filial devotion to the grumbling, slightly bilious, and preoccupied father figure. He is the force behind the "great man," the catalyst who receives none of the credit—a grown-up Tom Sawyer gone off to war. This is, of course, a literary type of long standing. Osbon is Jeeves, Jiminy Cricket, and Radar O'Reilly all rolled into one. And he isn't done yet.

Just as the *Hartford*, decks awash in blood, managed to get above Fort St. Philip, it encountered its greatest challenge. Employing an inventiveness born of desperation, the Confederates had constructed fire rafts, floating bonfires that they sent downstream in an attempt to ignite the Union's wooden frigates. Such a raft, directed by a tug, now descended upon the *Hartford*. In his zeal to elude it, the warship's pilot ran aground on a mud bank just above the smaller fort, but still within range of its guns. The flames ignited the ship's new coat of black paint and swelled to a height halfway up the rigging. In minutes the *Hartford* had become a raging inferno, and it was still being shelled by the guns of Fort St. Philip.

In popular accounts of the incident, Farragut rallies his men with the words: "Don't flinch from the fire, boys, there's a hotter fire for those who don't do their duty," and "Give that rascally tug a shot!" It seems unlikely under the circumstances that those were Farragut's exact words. More probable is the recollection of Lieutenant Albert Kautz, who saw Farragut raise his clasped hands in a gesture of anguish and exclaim, "My God, is it to end this way?"

Perhaps Farragut said all these things, but Osbon is silent on the matter. Instead, the clerk focuses the action on a curious, solitary figure, head and shoulders shrouded by a cloak, kneeling over something on the main deck. It is, of course, himself. With the cloak protecting him from the intense heat that is about to consume the ship, he is working furiously at a critical task. When Farragut sees him, he barks out a reprimand: "Come Mr. Osbon, this is no time for prayer." But the resourceful clerk is not praying. Instead he is *prying*, removing the caps from three 20-pound shells he has just brought on deck. He has managed to pry the last one off just as Farragut appears. "Flag Officer," he responds, "if you'll wait a second you'll get the quickest answer to prayer you ever heard of." With that he rolls the shells over the side and onto the fire raft, causing an explosion that promptly sinks it, allowing the men to extinguish the blaze on board. The pilot then backs the ship off the bank, and the *Hartford* slogs on to its next appointment with destiny.

History Repeats Itself

Naval history has left B. S. Osbon in its wake. A few of Farragut's biographers have chosen to acknowledge him, if only to add some color to the proceedings, but otherwise he seems doomed to remain one of the forgotten great men of American history. He is an interesting character, but clearly no match for the first admiral in the United States Navy, a man who assumed command of his first ship at the tender age of eleven (although quite unexpectedly and due to extenuating circumstances), and who in his sixties, suffering from poor eyesight, rheumatism, and possibly gout, and a little too fond of good food and drink, gave the Union something to cheer about.

What Osbon succeeds in showing is that David Farragut possessed qualities shared by some of the greatest military commanders of all time: calmness under fire, the ability to survey the entire field of battle, a knack for saying the right thing at the right time, an apparent lack of regard for personal safety, a reluctance to back down from a challenge, and finally, an apparent invulnerability. The portrait seems genuine enough; the artist, however, looks like a fake. It doesn't take an expert to detect this. All it takes is a slight familiarity with some of the more insistent motifs of battle narratives. To take one glaring example, consider Osbon's emphasis on Farragut's apparent invulnerability. The fact that the flag officer was lucky enough never to have been hit by shot or shell, when given the Osbon treatment, becomes a quality of Napoleonic dimension, an uncanny ability to cheat death.

Like any student of military history, Osbon would have known that Napoleon also constantly exposed himself to fire, to the exasperation of his own attendants. In his memoirs this illusion of invulnerability jumps out as a persistent and carefully cultivated theme, the emperor as a man of destiny who consistently avoids death by the narrowest of margins. At Arcis-sur-Aube in 1814, he rode his mount directly over a spinning, smoldering howitzer shell that had just burrowed into the mud. When it exploded, disemboweling his horse, it left the hero miraculously intact. At Essling in 1809 his Imperial Guard ordered him back out of the range of the guns, going so far as to threaten to lay down their arms if he refused. At Montereau in 1814 the Guard again reproved him for exposing himself on the front. His reply was characteristically immodest: "Fear not, the bullet that will kill me has not yet been cast." If he had known of it, he would undoubtedly have stolen a line from Charles V, the Holy Roman Emperor, who punctuated his refusal to remain in the rear at the Battle of Mühlberg in 1547 with the outburst: "Name me an emperor who was ever struck by a cannon ball!"

Military history is studded with such legends; they serve as recurrent motifs that historians use to establish a heroic lineage. Farragut, for example, was most often compared to Admiral Horatio Nelson, the hero of Trafalgar. Such a comparison was natural; Farragut first went to sea only five years after Nelson's glorious death. By the time he assumed command of the *Hartford*, the Union was looking for a Nelson of its own. In little episodes like the one that follows, they found one.

At the siege of Port Hudson in June of 1863, Lieutenant Winfield Scott Schley, one of Farragut's commanders, kept firing on the Confederate fortifications in spite of a cease-fire signal flag that hung limply from the masthead of the *Hartford*. Afterward, when Schley reported to the quarterdeck of the flagship, Farragut took him to task: "Captain, you begin early in your life to disobey orders. Did you not see the signal flying for nearly an hour to withdraw from action?" Schley tried to say something about the dead calm that made the flags difficult to read, but Farragut cut him off, saying, "I want none of this Nelson business in my squadron about not seeing signals." Schley knew very well what this "Nelson business" was. Every navy man did.

At Copenhagen in 1801, in the first naval action of the Napoleonic Wars, Nelson had stormed the harbor with twelve ships while his commander-in-chief, Admiral Sir Hyde Parker, kept another eight ships back as a reserve. A fierce firefight ensued, pitting Nelson against the moored Danish fleet and a series of shore batteries. Looking on from his distant vantage, Parker decided to choose discretion over valor and hoisted the signal for Nelson to withdraw. When the signal was pointed out to him, however, Nelson merely clapped his telescope to his blind eye and declared he could not see any signal. He then kept up the assault until the Danes gave in. The story stands to this day as one of the finest examples of reckless gallantry in the British navy. In reality it was nothing but a charade. Parker had previously sent a private message to the effect that Nelson could consider the order to withdraw optional and carry on the engagement as he saw fit. Parker had merely intended to give Nelson a way out if he needed it. He didn't. The stunt with the telescope had been a bit of stage business, a joke.

In the Port Hudson incident, the roles were reversed. The great man reprimanded his subordinate, then led him down to his cabin where he dropped all formality and revealed the joke. "I have censured you, sir, on the quarterdeck for what appeared to be a disregard of my orders," Farragut said. "I desire now to commend you and your officers and men for doing what you believed to be right under the circumstances. Do it again whenever in your judgment it is necessary to carry out your conception of duty. Will you take a glass of wine, sir?"

I Buy a Chinese Family and Join a Pirate Brig

In the history of warfare uncanny coincidences, parallels, and recurrent themes crop up with such regularity that it is difficult to know what to believe. History does repeat itself in a variety of ways, and coincidences alone are not enough to undermine the credibility of B. S. Osbon. But a quick glance through his "as told to" memoir, *A Sailor of Fortune*, gives the game away. For a book listed by some otherwise diligent Farragut biographers as a primary source, one that many Civil War writers quote indiscriminately, Osbon's story looks and reads suspiciously like a Horatio Alger novel. The chapter titles (including such eye-catchers as "I Buy a Chinese Family and Join a Pirate Brig," "I Meet the Prince of Wales and Enjoy His Friendship," "I Become Part of the Mexican Problem," and "I Have Dealings with Napoleon III") raise a few red flags. From his account of befriending Abraham Lincoln to the tips he provides for ship designer John Ericsson on how to improve his *Monitor*, we feel we are in the hands of a master yarn spinner, but not a reliable eyewitness to history.

Osbon did exist and filed stories (actually the same story) on Farragut for the *New York Herald* and *Harper's Weekly*, which seem to provide most of the facts about New Orleans that Albert Bigelow Paine inserted into *A Sailor of Fortune*. But when we take into account Paine's other literary output (some 50 works ranging from biographies to poetry to children's stories) alongside his weak claim to have set Osbon's story down "from the lips of the narrator," we begin to understand why a few (but only a few) of Farragut's biographers have ignored Osbon entirely. It could very well be that Paine was taken in by an impostor. Did Farragut really say "Damn the glasses"? We have only Paine's word for it, and, to be truthful, in Paine's book the words are spoken not by Farragut, but by Osbon. Most writers who use the story either do not check this fact or choose to ignore it, leaving the reader to draw the conclusion that Farragut's more famous words were the result of a rhetorical tic, as though we might reasonably infer the following dialogue:

"Sir, there is an eagle overhead."

"Damn the eagle!"

"But Flag Officer, the opera glasses."

"Damn the glasses!"

"Sir, I think that fire raft is heading for us."

"Damn the fire raft!"

"But sir, there are TORPEDOES in the harbor!"

"WHAT? Goddamn it!"

David Farragut never claimed to have said, "Damn the torpedoes." The claim was made for him fourteen years after the Battle of Mobile Bay (which occurred two years after the Battle of New Orleans), and eight years after Farragut's death. Moreover, as we will see in Chapter 11, the occasion of that remark was not a point of pride for him. If he could have rewritten history, Farragut would have made certain not to be obliged to make the comment in the first place.

Osbon tells us (through Albert Bigelow Paine) that Farragut's chief characteristic was to follow orders, that when he made history at Mobile Bay, he was simply doing his duty. "Before all," Osbon says, "he was a sailor in the service of his country and he let nothing stand between him and victory." To which he added, "I can understand how he looked there, and just how his voice sounded when he said, 'Damn the torpedoes! Go ahead on the engines!' I have seen the look and I have

17

heard the voice—and . . . I never fail to recall the night between the forts, and I lift my hat in honor of the man to whom death was nothing—to whom his nation's cause was all."

What should we make of this? It would be going too far to say that history always lies. Better to say that it invents to fill a need: the need for national sagas and for heroes who inspire pride and serve as role models. Such stories build esprit de corps, instill patriotism, and provide lessons in leadership. As historical devices, fighting words preserve the memory of fighting men, and thus can motivate other men to action—to fight, to press on, to vigilantly fall back, to resolve to conquer or die. Yet when historical narratives soar too high, they can easily lose touch with the hearts and minds they are supposed to inspire. Over time, "Damn the torpedoes" has suffered such a fate: the phrase is now so completely removed from Farragut, Mobile Bay, and the Civil War that it no longer connects with us in the way it was intended to.

This is a problem with military history in general. It is rarely impartial. What strikes the winning side as glorious and praiseworthy is unlikely to impress the losing side. Each side will produce very different versions of events, and with the passage of time, as memories of the rivalry fade away, what remain are tales of feats of arms that ring false and diminish the deeds they were intended to praise. In the chapters that follow I try to correct this tendency so that by the final chapter, when it will at last be explained, the title of this book will ring more true.

Who will follow me? Who is brave? Who will be the first to lay his man low?

King Cyrus
To his Persian infantry
6th century BC

Paradise is under the shadow of our swords. Forward.

Caliph Omar Ibn Al-khattab
Battle of Kadisiya

Come on, come on! What do ye, sirs? Lay on, lay on.

Taillefer, a Norman minstrel
Leading the charge at the Battle of Hastings
14 October 1066

Order of the Genoese forward, and begin the battle in the name of God and St. Denis.

King Philip VI of France
Battle of Crécy
26 August 1346

Men, remember, there is no retreat from here. You must die where you stand.

Sir Colin Campbell
To the 93rd British Highlanders
Battle of Balaclava (Crimean War)
25 October 1854

Cavalry to advance and take advantage of any opportunity to recover the Heights.

Lord Raglan
To the Light Brigade
Battle of Balaclava
25 October 1854

"The Thin Red Line" at the Battle of Balaclava, from a painting of that name by William Gibb. The distance between the Highlanders and the Russian cavalry is greatly diminished for effect.

CHAPTER TWO

Charge, and Give No Foot of Ground!

GOING OVER THE TOP AT BALACLAVA

The Charge

On the fifth of November in 1757, in the second year of the Seven Years' War, a vastly outnumbered Prussian army commanded by Frederick the Great took on a combined French and Austrian force outside the small village of Rossbach in Saxony, just west of Leipzig. On Frederick's left wing, his cavalry commander, General Friedrich von Seydlitz, leading some 4000 horsemen, noticed the enemy attempting a surprise infantry maneuver on that flank. Without waiting for orders, Seydlitz led his men forward at a trot. Then, spurring his horse to a canter, he placed himself in full view of the entire line of proud hussars, who hung on his every gesture, awaiting the signal to attack. It wasn't long in coming. By way of letting them know, Seydlitz nonchalantly tossed his tobacco pipe into the air, and they charged off to victory.

History serves up many instances of spontaneous charges, of throwaway gestures such as Seydlitz's, and, of course, of timely delivered words of inspired flamboyance—grand, if not grandstanding, expressions such as, "Fix bayonets and go for them!" and *"Tout le monde a la bataille!"* ["All hands into battle!"] At the Battle of Ivry during the French religious wars of the late sixteenth century, King Henry IV is reported to have spurred his Huguenot cavalry to attack with the words, "I am your king. You are a Frenchman. There is the enemy. Charge!"

General Winfield Scott goaded his men into battle at Chippewa, Canada in 1814 with the challenge, "The enemy say that Americans are good at a long shot, but cannot stand the cold iron. I call upon you to give lie to the slander. Charge!"

Taking such accounts at face value, it is easy to come away with the impression that in all battles both men and horses are chafing at the bit, some literally, some figuratively. Poised on the brink of warlike frenzy, it takes only a nod or a wink to send them over the edge, over the top, off to the chase, or out on a bloody rampage. Hollywood directors and screenwriters have done their share in promoting this image—the battle as Oklahoma land rush, as buffalo stampede, or as head-on train wreck. This is also the favored treatment of war in art and literature, two massed forces of brave hearts throwing themselves at each other with unbridled fury, driven by thoughts of God, country, family, duty, loyalty, honor, sacrifice, and possibly even a lust for blood, money, or revenge. Typically, at the focal point of the action, two gallant commanders cry out the order to attack, each flourishing a sword and pointing the way to victory.

The problem with this scenario is that it has rarely happened on a real battlefield. Battles of the glorious past did feature charges and countercharges; that much is not disputed. What they rarely produced, however, was head-on collisions, an event so unheard of that Frederick the Great used to guarantee his men that if they merely closed with the enemy, they would not have to fight; the enemy would simply abandon its position. This is what happened at Rossbach.

War, as Frederick came to understand it, consisted of feints, thrusts, and parries, executed with more style than substance, and the order to charge was rarely followed through to its conclusion. Witness Louis-Adolphe Thiers, a nineteenth-century French historian who pointed out that in one of Napoleon's battles: "The Russians behaved courageously and, *what seldom happens in war*, two bodies of infantry were seen marching resolutely against each other without either of them giving way before meeting." It simply wasn't done. Two forces might advance on each other, but long before they came within lethal range, one side or the other usually pulled up. Sometimes both did.

This is not what we have been conditioned to believe, but it is an observation that, once stated, makes immediate sense. Many of us find it hard to resist a good battle scene from the golden era of Hollywood epics, but it comes as something of a relief to hear that such things never took place as reenacted for the cameras. It is easier to accept the idea that while soldiers can be led anywhere on a drill field, they cannot easily be induced to rush headlong to collide with an advancing enemy. Unlike two football teams at the kickoff, infantry and cavalry regiments do not seek out collisions. (The horsemen may be willing, but the horses are too smart for that.) It is true that cavalry regiments lived to charge, but in battle they would do so only when they had a chance of infiltrating or scattering an opposing force, and never to the point of collision. This explains why a crush of cavalry against cavalry has never been recorded except on a few canvases in the Louvre and the Metropolitan Museum. The same is true of infantry battles: the image of two hordes rushing upon one another with bayonets flashing is a romantic invention. The reality is characterized by caution and trepidation, a fact suggested by the Greek historian Xenophon when he describes Cyrus, the sixth-century BC Persian king, leading his infantry against Assyrian charioteers with the words: "Who will follow me? Who is brave? Who will be the first to lay his man low?" Who indeed! Yet most representations of battle—artistic, cinematic, and literary—manage to get it all wrong, and in doing so obscure a crucial tenet of military strategy: that the display of force is more feasible than the application of it.

The Battle Studies of Charles Ardant du Picq

As a military theorist, Charles Ardant du Picq, a colonel of the French infantry during the Franco-Prussian War of 1870, explained all of this more than a century ago, but his observations have been overshadowed by those of his more famous contemporaries. Du Picq, for example, has more useful things to say about the behavior of men in battle than does his more celebrated predecessor, Karl von Clausewitz. Du Picq distilled years of careful reading and considerable on-the-job observation into a handy volume entitled *Battle Studies*, which is less quoted than Clausewitz's ubiquitous *On War* partly because du Picq's conclusions are more resistant to misinterpretation. While Clausewitz waxes philosophical about moral force and collective will ("War is an act of force to compel our adversary to do our will."), du Picq focuses on the agents of that will who must apply the actual force—that is, on the men who have to do the fighting. His conclusion, while logical, if not crucial to understanding warfare, is not exactly sublime. According to du Picq, "Man does not enter battle to fight, but for victory. He does everything he can do to avoid the first and obtain the second." This is probably the single most important factor determining the course of any fight ever waged.

Du Picq contended that prior to the modern era, head-to-head battles were relatively rare events and that commanders tried to avoid them. They conducted sieges, countersieges, and raids and employed stealth whenever possible, always seeking the path of least resistance. Even when armies met on equal terms (and even when they did not), their commanders made every effort to achieve either surprise, by executing flanking maneuvers (such as Frederick's celebrated "oblique order"), or shock, by making cavalry charges or rapid deployments of infantry troops in order to confuse the enemy, demoralize him, and send him into a panic.

The exception to the rule was Greek phalanx warfare, which historian Victor Davis Hanson has called the "Western way of war," but with considerable irony, for the Greek Warrior was an anomaly. In the era of Greece's preeminence, the fifth century BC, Greek armored infantry forces met head to head and engaged in what were, essentially, massive shoving matches. Tactics were minimal. No attempt was made to outflank or surprise the opposition, and the more determined side usually won. This form of Homeric struggle left a lasting impression on historians, if not on Hollywood writers and directors, who sustained the memory of the long-extinct Greek way of war (the "Western way") by grafting it onto every subsequent era. On film, Celts and Brits, crusaders and infidels, Russians and Mongols, cowboys and Indians collide in a writhing and seething crush of murderous mayhem, the open field equivalent of a barroom brawl.

A close reading of military history reveals a different picture. With the decline of the Greek phalanx, the introduction of more lethal weaponry, and the perfection of new methods of killing from a distance, the head-on clash of armies gradually gave way to the art of maneuver. In his later campaigns, Frederick the Great's strategy (according to Major General Henry Lloyd) boiled down to this: "Initiate military operations with mathematical precision and keep waging war without ever being under the necessity to strike a blow." In other words, do whatever is necessary to win a war of attrition without engaging the enemy directly. Maurice de Saxe, one of the great eighteenth-century French generals, agreed. "I do not favor battles, particularly at the beginning of a war," he wrote. "I am sure a good general can make war all his life and not be compelled to fight one." Von Seydlitz himself admitted as much when he conceded that the cavalry wins battles not with the saber but with the riding whip.

This helps to explain Abraham Lincoln's exasperation with the Union Army leadership, in particular with George McClellan's policy of waging a war of attrition. His eventual successor, Ulysses S. Grant, may have been criticized for sacrificing thousands of men in battles of unprecedented carnage, but as Lincoln said in his defense, "I cannot spare this man, he fights." It was not simply a compliment, but a confirmation that actual fighting was necessary, and that his other generals, students of European warfare, had been reluctant to do it.

Grant understood that what really matters in battle is sustained fire power and the will to advance deliberately, no matter what the cost. He also knew that getting an army to do this was no easy task. Lofty ideals may inspire men to join armies and march off to fields of battle; drums, bugles, and even unintelligible yells may set them into motion; but once they came face to face with the enemy, they rarely clashed at close quarters. One side or both would usually pause, and either dig in or turn around and head back. And no words, however finely crafted, could alter this.

The Charge of the Light Brigade

The preceding overview, compressing two millennia into a few pages as it does, overgeneralizes, but not outrageously. Its point is that any battle narrative should be scoured for evidence of reluctance under fire. For example, one of the best illustrations of the less than glorious reality of war is the Battle of Balaclava in 1854, an incident of the Crimean War distinguished by several cavalry charges and capped off by the infamous charge of the Light Brigade. Balaclava inspired a great deal of gushing prose and poetry that tends to disguise the fact that this event, like all battles of the distant past, was a chaotic affair in which cowardice and timidity played just as big a role as courage and audacity. But nothing had quite as much impact on the event as stupidity.

It is tempting to accept the famous sideline remark made by the French general Pierre Bosquet that, "It is magnificent, but it is not war." But the charge of the Light Brigade was indeed war at its best and worst. The over-quoted remark merely glossed over what the *London Times*'s man at the scene captured more accurately with the words "someone had blundered," a phrase lifted verbatim by Alfred Lord Tennyson in his "Charge of the Light Brigade" and elevated to a figure of speech. Blunder or not, the story behind the charge reminds us that the reality of war is not as glorious as we may have been led to believe, but is nonetheless interesting because it is all too human.

The Crimean War of 1854 is generally dismissed as a trivial episode born of political stupidity and nurtured by military incompetence. The British Cabinet authorized this unnecessary war during a meeting that most of its members slept through. The triggering episode, a Russian incursion into Turkish lands, had already been repulsed by the Turks; yet the British and French seized upon this pretext to launch an assault on the Black Sea peninsula that gave the war its name. This exercise in colonial posturing would be almost entirely forgotten were it not for two things: Florence Nightingale's band of nurses, who alleviated the suffering of British troops mired in trenches through a Russian winter that caught them unprepared, and one of the most famous of all war poems, which begins with these stirring lines:

> Half a league, half a league,
> Half a league onward,
> All in the valley of Death
> Rode the six hundred.

As such poems go, this one happens to be surprisingly factual. Tennyson doesn't shy away from acknowledging that this was a fiasco, but he doesn't do it complete justice either. For one thing, he fails to mention that it was the final charge of the day and the only one that ended badly for the British, or that the infamous charge had the unintended effect of wrenching defeat from the jaws of a standoff. The charge was made against the Russians, by the way, who sometimes go forgotten in all of the fuss. They would probably have been happy to forget the whole thing themselves, but they were the victors, and it is worth considering the event from their point of view.

The day had begun quite well for the Russians. After weeks of inactivity during which they found themselves entrenched in the Crimean port of Sevastopol, with the allied

English and French holding the nearby town of Balaclava to the south, the Russians decided upon a bold offensive aimed at taking four allied artillery redoubts manned mostly by Turks. These constituted the first line of defense for Balaclava. The batteries were unprepared and held out only for an hour or so before one bastion broke and ran, and the rest quickly followed. Cossack horsemen pursued the Turks, but by then the British lines had begun to form. The Russian cavalry then formed up as well.

Lieutenant General I.I. Ryzhov, a veteran of the Napoleonic Wars, commanded the hussar, uhlan, and Cossack regiments that formed the first wave of the Russian attack. Opposing him a mile away to the south stood the 93rd Highlanders, a regiment of kilted and red-coated Scots infantry deployed in a long, double line. Their commander, Sir Colin Campbell, reportedly gave his last instructions to the regiment by saying, "Men, remember there is no retreat from here. You must die where you stand." Whether he actually said this or anyone heard it, it makes perfect sense. The British infantry knew from the Peninsular Campaign (their defense of Spain against Napoleon's juggernaut) that if they could merely hold their ground, the enemy would do the retreating.

Both sides had their artillery in place. Not yet fully deployed but supporting the Highlanders were the dragoons of the Heavy Brigade, commanded by Brigadier General J.Y. Scarlett. Unlike Ryzhov, Scarlett would enjoy the advantage of seeing the action unfold. The Russian commander, however, could see neither the Highlanders, who had been positioned on the downslope of a hillock and ordered to lie down so as to avoid the Russian artillery fire, nor the full extent of the British cavalry, which also included Lord Cardigan's Light Brigade.

The charge of Ryzhov's uhlans got off to a bad start when the Ural Cossacks, on their own authority, decided to join in at a gallop, while the uhlans tried to maintain a trot. This is the most difficult aspect of a charge, whether of cavalry or infantry: if the men cannot maintain a uniform pace, the formation will come apart and its impact will be blunted. Ryzhov attempted to restore some discipline, but it must have been difficult under the fire of British case shot. Even more disruptive, however, was the sudden appearance of the Highlanders, who stood up en masse as the Russians drew within several hundred yards, and let them have it with a volley. The charge instantly ground to a halt.

Ryzhov would later claim that he had ordered the halt in order to redeploy his disrupted line. Although this saves some face for the Russians, it does not cover up their subsequent failure to rally. What it does do is to confirm du Picq's characterization of cavalry charges as threats in which the most threatening win. The Cossacks in particular had a fearsome reputation, but it had been earned mostly by their enthusiasm for chasing down fleeing men and brutally killing them. Ryzhov knew that they were undependable and that because their principal motivation was plunder they would back down in the face of a considerable show of force. As for the British infantry, they had inherited from their predecessors in the Napoleonic Wars a legacy of not flinching before artillery or cavalry—a sometimes suicidal determination that nonetheless won battles such as Albuera and Waterloo.

What we know of this event comes mostly from the British side. The Crimean War was the first war to be reported on a day-to-day basis by the press. Fueled by the exploits of Wellington's army a half-century earlier, the British press in particular did their best to help sustain the regimental legends. At Balaclava they were represented by William Howard Russell of the *Times*, who filed this eyewitness report:

> The Russians drew breath for a moment, and then in one grand line dashed at the Highlanders. The ground flies beneath their horses' feet; gathering speed at every stride, they dash on toward that thin red streak topped with a line of steel . . . . But ere they come within 150 yards, another deadly volley flashes from leveled rifle, and carries death and terror into the Russians.

As more than one observer has noted, the British are particularly adept at turning regimental history into legend, and this is an excellent specimen. Russell's inspired prose has had a great influence on subsequent writers. Tennyson, for example, based both "The Charge of the Light Brigade" and its companion piece, the lesser-known "Charge of the Heavy Brigade," on Russell's report. Others plucked "the thin red line" out of the second sentence and made it the signature of the British infantry, inspiring such spin-offs as "the long gray line" to describe the cadets of West Point. In this instance, a day that resulted in a net loss for the British inspired more memorable war writing than all but a handful of battles in all of history. With the halt of the Russian charge, of course, the day had only just begun.

As the Russian horsemen stood frozen in their indecision, Lord Raglan, the commander of the British forces, called for a countercharge, which Scarlett delivered with his Heavy Brigade. Timed just as the Russians were at the height of disorganization, this threat proved overwhelming. Although far outnumbered by the Russian cavalry, Scarlett's men drove among the foe and began slashing with their swords. The Russians fled. "In forty-two years of service and ten campaigns, among them Kulm, Leipzig, and Paris," wrote Ryzhov afterwards, "never have I seen such action, with both sides cutting and thrusting at each other for so long." But Ryzhov's recollection is self-serving: the action lasted less than ten minutes, during which time his men were completely routed. While the Russians accounted for eight British dead and about seventy wounded, they suffered three to four times that number of casualties themselves and were driven from the field. Meanwhile Cardigan's Light Brigade could only look on with impatience. Lord Raglan refused to send them in pursuit, and both sides regrouped.

Although a nice illustration of some of du Picq's theories, if not of the techniques employed by war correspondents and generals to describe an action well after the fact, all this is merely prologue to the main event. It was still morning and the Russians may have assumed that the day's fighting was done, but the British had other ideas. Having lost four artillery redoubts and incensed at the sight of Russians preparing to dismantle and remove his guns, Lord Raglan was now ready to set in motion a series of miscommunications that would result in one of the more glorious disasters on record.

Helmuth von Moltke, who was appointed chief of the Prussian general staff at about this time, may well have been thinking of the Battle of Balaclava when he announced to his retinue, "Remember, gentlemen, an order that can be misunderstood will be misunderstood." The charge of the Light Brigade was a textbook case of Moltke's (or Murphy's) law of command in action. Here is how it unfolded.

From his hilltop vantage, Lord Raglan surveyed the outcome of the morning's action. Piqued by the loss of the guns, he issued the following order to Lord Lucan, the commander of the British cavalry: "Cavalry to advance and take advantage of any opportunity to recover the Heights. They will be supported by the infantry, which have been ordered to advance on two fronts." It was a profoundly confusing message given that Lucan, in the valley below, did not enjoy his commander's field of view and had no idea of the opportunity presented by the redoubts. Assuming that he was supposed to wait for infantry support, and seeing none, he did nothing.

Half an hour later Raglan was fuming. He could see the Russians now at work, removing the guns and vulnerable to a charge. But Lord Lucan was oblivious to the source of Raglan's frustration. All he could see was the Don Cossack field battery well over a mile away to the southeast, at the head of a causeway flanked by two other Russian artillery batteries. Raglan, nearly apoplectic, then fired off another order that merely added to the confusion caused by the last: "Lord Raglan wishes the cavalry to advance rapidly to the front. Follow the enemy and try to prevent the enemy from carrying away the guns. Troops Horse Artillery may accompany. French cavalry is on

31

your left. Immediate." He entrusted the delivery of this fateful missive to Captain Lewis Edward Nolan, an impetuous officer known more for his superior horsemanship than for his common sense. As Nolan sped off, Raglan yelled to him, "Tell Lord Lucan the cavalry is to attack immediately."

Lucan was even more perplexed by this new order. He had no idea what it meant. Turning in exasperation to the equally exasperated messenger, he sputtered, "What guns? Where and what to do?" To which Nolan, himself impatient for action, merely compounded the problem by waving vaguely in the direction of the redoubts, shouting, "*There*, my Lord! *There* is your enemy! *There* are your guns." Too flustered to use up more time seeking clarification, Lucan passed the order on to Cardigan, who thought it to be suicidal but was told there was no choice but to obey.

All this time Nolan remained blissfully unaware of the mix-up in objectives and placed himself squarely in the front ranks of the Light Brigade, a place he had no authority to be. Just as the charge got under way he must have realized that something was wrong, that someone had indeed blundered, and it just might have been himself. According to some witnesses, Nolan cut in front from left to right, apparently trying too late to redirect the charge toward the proper objective. But the Russian artillery had just opened up and a shell fragment caught Nolan in the midsection. He fell to the ground in agony. Thus, with their resolve firmly pointed in the wrong direction, the 673 men of the Light Brigade, minus Nolan, their first to fall, rode off to dubious fame.

Even though misdirected and ill-advised, the charge of the Light Brigade was not ineffective. Shock would be the appropriate word to describe the reaction of the Russians, who no more expected a charge through that particular valley than they expected an unconditional surrender. Their artillerymen, who were never flustered, went immediately into action, and their guns took a terrible toll among the horsemen. But the brigade could not be stopped. The sight of it inspired General

Bosquet, the French commander observing the event from the hilltop with Lord Raglan, to make his famous remark that while it was magnificent, it was not war. But it is his rarely quoted follow-up remark that more accurately sums up the event. "It is folly," he said. Yet for the Russians in its path it was deadly serious business.

All this time General Ryzhov, standing at the Don Cossack field battery, was blissfully unaware of what was happening. As he meandered about the seemingly secure Russian lines, his attention was drawn to a distant cloud of dust that began to loom larger and larger down the causeway. The general at first looked with astonishment, and then with the growing realization that this was a British cavalry regiment, and it was headed directly at him. Orders were shouted, the Don Cossack battery leapt into action and opened fire, but nothing seemed capable of stopping that charge. When Ryzhov tried to deploy his Cossacks, he got nowhere. They were completely unnerved. As one of Ryzhov's aides later wrote:

> The Cossacks, frightened by the disciplined order of the mass of cavalry bearing down on them, did not hold, but, wheeling to their left, began to fire on their own troops in their efforts to clear a route of escape . . . the whole of the Russian cavalry force in the valley made off, the good officers trying in vain to hold their men—some threw themselves forward against the enemy only to be cut down—General Ryzhov being one of the last to withdraw, seeking death, for he knew he would be held responsible.

When the Light Brigade, or what was left of it, at last reached the battery, they began slashing at the gunners and spiking the guns, and even tried to drag some field pieces away. Others continued to pursue the Russian horsemen, who were desperately trying to flee over a bridge. A Russian artillery officer filed this account:

There, in a small area at the exit of the gorge, were four Russian horse regiments stampeding around, and inside this mass, in small isolated patches, were the redcoated English, probably no less surprised than ourselves how unexpectedly this had happened. The enemy soon came to the conclusion that they had nothing to fear from hussars or Cossacks and, tired of slashing, they decided to return the way they had come through another cannonade of artillery and rifle fire. . . . With such desperate courage, these valiant lunatics set off again, and not one of the living—even the wounded—surrendered.

The Russian cavalry were too unnerved to do anything for a long time, but as the same officer notes, the Cossacks were the first to recover and, "true to their nature, they set themselves to the task at hand—rounding up English horses and offering them for sale."

Meanwhile the returning English faced the gauntlet again, only this time with better odds. The French Chasseurs d'Afrique had set off after them and swung left to take out the Russian battery on the Fedioukine hills. They had also been joined by the Heavy Brigade. But casualties were heavy. Of the 673 who set out, about 200 returned intact. Many more had been dismounted and struggled back on foot. In all, 113 were listed as killed and 134 wounded. By the time it was over, the Light Brigade was effectively lost as a fighting unit, a point that Lord Raglan impressed on Lord Lucan with bitter reproachfulness. At the cost of an effective force of almost 700, which had been cut to half its strength, the British managed to take out a single Russian field battery. Even the Heavy Brigade, which had performed so brilliantly that morning, suffered significant losses.

The entire fiasco had no tactical significance. The Russian line advanced somewhat; the allies established a new defensive line and so held on to Balaclava. The principal result of the charge of the Light Brigade was that from then on the Russians regarded the British cavalry as reckless madmen who were capable of anything, but Raglan would not be able to take advantage of this. In the end, the British and French allies won the war, a fact that seems almost incidental.

A charge can be a form of bluffing, but a better analogy, in light of Balaclava, is the game of chicken, in which two sides rush upon each other with the object of seeing who will flinch first. Du Picq cites an incident, also from the Crimean War, in which two opposing detachments, "coming around one of the mounds of earth that covered the country and meeting unexpectedly face to face, stopped thunderstruck. Then, forgetting their rifles, they threw stones and withdrew." It sounds absurd. At the very least, it is at odds with what we have been led to believe about war. Yet this type of behavior turns up with regularity in some of the more candid memoirs of battle. The point is that a lot of what we think of as fighting consists of *not* fighting, but merely threatening to. The American Civil War (and presumably many other wars) featured several episodes in which one side succeeded in "yelling" the other side out of position. Although not as dramatic as a cavalry charge, the effect is essentially the same. The threat of an attack often achieves more than a real attack would. It is the psychological rather than the physical damage inflicted that determines the outcome. This helps to explain why an army that refuses to admit it is beaten often cannot be beaten.

Goddamn it! Start shooting!

Lt. Colonel Robert G. Cole

At Carentan Causeway
Allied invasion of Normandy
10 June 1944

Hunde, wollt ihr ewig leben?
[Dogs, do you wish to live forever?]

Frederick the Great

Attributed remark to his Guards

C'mon, you sons of bitches, do you want to live forever?

Sergeant Dan Daly, USMC

Battle of Belleau Wood
6 June 1918

Grant me one step forward and we shall have victory.

Epameinondas, the Theban commander

Battle of Leuctra
371 BC

Goddamn it, you'll never get the Purple Heart hiding in a foxhole! Follow me!

Lt. Colonel Henry P. Crowe, USMC

Battle of Guadalcanal
13 January 1943

Frederick the Great urging on his guards at the Battle of Leuthen.

CHAPTER THREE

Fire at Will!

EXPLAINING SERGEANT YORK

Reluctance under Fire

During the Second World War, the General Staff of the United States Army established a historical division in order to compile an exhaustive history of the war. They staffed it with military men, some of them veterans of World War I, with impressive journalistic credentials. Among those who shipped out to document the war in the Pacific was Samuel Lyman Atwood Marshall, a veteran newsman who went by his initials and was affectionately known as "Slam." A lieutenant in the American Expeditionary Force in 1918, he was promoted to lieutenant colonel for his new assignment, which began with the invasion of the Marshall and Solomon Islands in 1943.

Although he was supposed to look at the big picture, Marshall had a soft spot for firsthand testimony, the closer to the action the better. By putting himself in harm's way, he was able to debrief soldiers in the immediate aftermath of firefights. Before long, he discovered that no two participants in the same action told the same story, and it was not simply a difference in perspective. Impressions differed so much that Marshall found it difficult to piece together exactly what had taken place. The men themselves did not seem to know what they were caught up in. War stories, Marshall discovered, tend to settle into logical narratives with the passage of time, once the participants have had the chance to share and compare their experiences. But these soldiers, so fresh from battle that they had not yet been able to process the sensation of it, were telling Marshall something unexpected, and the novelty of it would blossom into a consuming passion for the newsman. Marshall would devote the rest of his professional life to understanding the actions, reactions, and inactions of men under fire. After his stint in the Pacific, Marshall took this quest to Europe, where he became the official historian of that war, and much later he would do the same in Korea and Vietnam.

Although he may not have realized it at the time, Marshall was following in the footsteps of Charles Ardant du Picq, who had collected similar testimonies by circulating questionnaires among his fellow officers. Marshall concentrated on the rank and file, and used a team of researchers to interview soldiers fresh from combat, before they had a chance to sort it all out. From such raw material, du Picq and Marshall arrived at some surprising conclusions that have since become famous among war analysts, but not so well known among popular historians. What they discovered, among other things, was that even with dynamic leadership most men were reluctant to shoot to kill, even to save their own lives. Even more surprisingly, a large percentage were unwilling to shoot at all.

In *Men Against Fire*, the book in which he published his findings and that is in many ways a twentieth-century counterpart of du Picq's *Battle Studies*, Marshall noted that most men are not natural fighters, and need constant direction and encouragement. "A commander of infantry," he wrote, "will be well advised to believe that when he engages the enemy not more than one quarter of his men will ever strike a real blow unless they are compelled by almost overpowering circumstance or unless all junior leaders constantly 'ride herd' on troops with the specific mission of increasing their fire." Not coincidentally, du Picq had come to the same conclusion almost a century earlier: "At a distance, numbers of troops without cohesion may be impressive, but up close they are reduced to fifty or twenty-five percent who really fight." Marshall illustrated the point with many stories that serve as contradictions to traditional battle narratives. Here is one of them.

During an action four days after the D-Day landings in Normandy, Lieutenant Colonel Robert G. Cole of the 502nd Parachute Infantry got his first chance to see how his men would react to the stress of being under fire. To his dismay, he discovered that they froze. Pinned down without adequate cover, Cole (who was later killed in action in Holland) risked exposure to enemy fire by moving up and down his column of men, trying desperately to get them to shoot.

> I found no way to make them continue to fire. Not one man in twenty-five voluntarily fired his weapon. There was no cover; they could not dig in. Therefore their only protection was to continue a fire which would make the enemy keep his head down. They had all been taught this principle in training. They all knew it very well. But they could not force themselves to act upon it. When I ordered the men who were right around me to fire, they did so. But the moment I passed on, they quit. I walked up and down the line yelling, "Goddamn it! Start shooting!" But it did little good. They fired only while I watched them or while some other officer stood over them.

In other instances, Marshall found troops such as these who would advance on the enemy, often undeterred by the danger, yet still they would not fire their weapons. During the course of his interviews with both green and experienced men, Marshall came to this simple, shocking conclusion: that in any infantry engagement no more than a quarter of the troops under fire shot back. That is, at least *three-quarters of those in action never fired their weapons at all.* They would stand up to the danger, but they would not fire their weapons. Even in engagements involving seasoned veterans, "on average not more than 15% fired at the enemy, where it had been possible for 80% to fire." Clearly, something more than inexperience or nervousness was at work.

41

It seems that Marshall had stumbled upon the great lie in all of military history and literature that asserts that the majority of men at war are ready, willing, and able to kill. The reality is more humbling and more human. The average soldier is as reluctant to kill as to be killed, if not more so. He will go to great lengths to avoid the risk of dying in battle, as one would expect, but surprisingly, a majority of soldiers will make an even greater effort to avoid killing someone else.

Marshall's conclusions, which were not initially well-received by the public or the military brass, require some qualification. He is not talking about artillery crews or machine gunners or elite corps of commandos. Nor is he talking about distance killing, in which one fires from long range at an unseen enemy or launches a missile as part of a massive volley from a safe vantage point; or about firing upon a helpless, fleeing, or incompetent opponent. He is, rather, talking about the average fighting Joe, caught up in the kind of face-to-face conflict that battle narratives tend to dwell upon: opposing lines of troops firing at each other, advancing lines of skirmishers storming an enemy stronghold, loose formations of foot soldiers advancing to meet a similar force in a clash of battalions. He also restricts his conclusions to modern (World War II era) armies, and thus to nonprofessionals—men who have come from everyday walks of life and intend to return there.

Even so, one is immediately tempted to extend Marshall's conclusions to armies of other eras. Could the reluctance to kill have been a factor in wars fought in the classical era or in medieval times? Were Colonel Cole's men any different in this respect from, for example, the Greek hoplites, the Roman centurions, the crusading knights, the Ottoman janissaries, or the British Redcoats? The technology of war makes such comparisons difficult. Deadlier weapons call forth more crippling fears, and the compositions of armies change from age to age—some are filled out by volunteers, others by mercenaries, others by conscripts, and still others by regulars—which affects their psychological make-up. But Marshall, for one, believed that this reluctance is natural and has always existed:

> Commanders in all ages have dealt with this central problem according to the weapons of their day and their imaginative employment of formations which would bring the maximum strength of those weapons to bear at the decisive point.

In other words, great generals of the past tried to reduce what is essentially a psychological problem to a geometrical one. Through the use of imaginative formations, rapid deployments, infantry-to-cavalry ratios, and other paper-and-pencil measures, they maneuvered their way around having to admit that most of their men simply did not share a taste for blood. They would willingly march off to war, advance into battle, and even face down the enemy, but in the final analysis most soldiers were simply unwilling or unable to go for the kill.

That the United States Army was not unique in this one regard is borne out by the literature of warfare. Although it takes some reading between the lines, proof of the individual soldier's reluctance to use his weapon and his inability to aim it can be found in the very tactics and orders that commanders have resorted to in every era. Some of the orders are so familiar as to be clichés. When Oliver Cromwell told his troops at the Battle of Marston Moor (in 1644) to "Trust in God and aim at their shoelaces," he betrays to us a fact all too familiar to him: that riflemen tend to shoot too high. When at the Battle of Prague in 1757 Frederick the Great ordered his men to withhold fire until they could see the whites of the enemy's eyes, he admitted his soldiers' exasperating propensity to fire too soon. When Sergeant Dan Daly yelled to his fellow Marines at Belleau Wood in 1918, "C'mon you sons of bitches, do you want to live forever?", he confirmed, among other things, that the bulk of the fighting effort falls to platoon leaders and other natural fighters, a small minority who have to exert tremendous force in order to get their men to follow and to fight. Isolating such phrases may create the impression that soldiers revel in simple rousing slogans, like so much ballfield chatter, and that they love to fight. But taken together, they demonstrate the opposite: that soldiers have always required constant direction and reassurance in battle in order to overcome their natural reluctance.

A Capsule History of Reluctance in Battle

Evidence of measures to contain man's fear of battle comes down to us from, among others, the ancient Greeks, who designed not just a battle formation but an entire ethic to accommodate those who were reluctant to kill. During the fifth century BC, the average Greek infantryman (or *hoplite*, as he is called) was not a professional soldier but an ordinary citizen serving alongside his brothers, his cousins, his neighbors, and his friends. When he went off to war, he was expected to take his place in the phalanx—a line of armored men at least three ranks deep. In the Greek battle formation each man wore a breastplate, greaves to protect the shins, and a bronze helmet. On his left he carried a massive shield braced on his shoulder, and in his right hand he wielded a spear. A bronze sword hung from his belt. Aligned with his comrades in one long shield-wall, the average Greek hoplite acknowledged fear as a fact of war, but not as something to be ashamed of as long as one stayed in the ranks. The natural fighters, a minority, were positioned in the front two ranks and did most of the killing. But Greek society was enlightened enough to reserve its highest accolades for those who merely backed them up. That is, the greatest virtue of the Greek hoplite was to swallow his fear and remain in the formation. As Socrates, a formidable phalanx fighter himself, put it, one "must stay put there and face the danger without any regard for death or anything else more than disgrace."

The Greek phalanx was nothing if not a pragmatic tactic: the immediate presence of comrades helped to stave off the panic that isolation can induce on the battlefield, and the formation did not require every man to be a killer. Each hoplite contributed simply by being there and moving forward, whether he directed a blow or not. The moral pressure to stand firm was intense. Each man knew that if one man broke, the whole of the line could be breached by the enemy. But if they held together and kept moving forward, the odds were with them. At the climax of the Battle of Leuctra in 371 BC, the Theban general Epameinondas gave a perfect illustration of the concept when, instead of the usual histrionics calling for the men to attack, fight, and kill in the name of duty, honor, and country, he simply said, "Grant me one step forward and we shall have victory." They did, and they won.

The Spartans, that most warlike of Greek tribes, are generally credited with inventing the phalanx in the seventh century BC. They probably did so because they recognized precisely what S.L.A. Marshall rediscovered 2500 years later. Given the technology of the weaponry of their day and the necessity of hand-to-hand fighting, the phalanx provided the Spartans a way to maximize the offensive potential of their traditionally small armies. No non-phalanx army could stand up to them. Marshall cites the example of Cyrus the Great, who, when told that the Egyptian battle formation was one hundred men deep, said, "If they are too deep to reach their enemies with their weapons, what good are they?" Ironically, this attitude explains why Persian kings never defeated a Greek phalanx on an open field. What Cyrus overlooked is that the massed formation helped to reduce the fear within its own ranks and instilled greater fear in the opposition. It also provided the means for filling the gaps created by those who fell, thus keeping the formation intact.

The Greek phalanx progressed through a variety of stages in the armies of later civilizations. While the massed formation incorporated new weapons and adopted more sophisticated deployments, it survived as an essential infantry tactic because of its utility—the phalanx maximized the threat of a mass of men even though the majority of its members were not very threatening. But in the Middle Ages the phalanx disappeared, to be supplanted by the one-on-one duel and the melee. Both were made possible by advancements in metallurgy.

The era of the phalanx gave way to the age of the knight, the so-called age of chivalry, in which battles played out like elaborate rituals with codes that strongly denounced flight from the battlefield. The transition to this form of warfare was gradual and was made possible by the development of armor light enough to allow knights to ride into battle with an illusion of invulnerability. This illusion was sustained as long as knights fought against similarly armed knights. Free to brawl, and protected from serious injury by a thin coat of metal, they could flail away unencumbered by thoughts of death, knowing that if things went badly, they could surrender and offer ransom or simply run away. Although a simplification of twelfth-century warfare (which featured few pitched battles), this picture of low-risk fighting is no myth. Philippe Contamine in *War in the Middle Ages* points out that in 1127, a year of war throughout Flanders involving about a thousand knights, a mere seven deaths were registered, four of them by accidents. Of the 900 knights who faced off at the Battle of Brémule in 1119, only three were killed. Du Picq weighs in with an example of his own: the celebrated Battle of the Thirty, as related by the medieval chronicler Froissart. The year was 1351 when the Maréchal de Beaumanoir led thirty Breton knights and squires against the same number of English in order to settle a feud. As du Picq notes with feigned astonishment, "The battle had lasted up to exhaustion without loss by the English!" When at long last it was over, only twelve men had been killed, four of them overcome with heat exhaustion brought on by their own armor.

All of this came to an end in the 1500s, when Swiss pikemen revived the phalanx and gunpowder technology rendered body armor useless. The mounted knight, sans armor, evolved into the cavalryman, the phalanx evolved into the modern infantry, and commanders had to adjust once again to the reality that killing is not a natural activity for most men. Now that those men carried rifles, the problem became one of using them to best effect. One solution relied on peer pressure. Because soldiers worked most effectively in massed formations and because they were more willing to fight in the company of others, it made sense to line them up and have them all fire at once. This solution was known as fire on command or fire by platoon. Another solution, chosen by Napoleon as the only practical one for a very large army, was the command to fire at will. But because most soldiers fired wildly, simply to relieve the stress of battle, many others fired without aiming, and many didn't fire at all, the field of honor was left open to a select group of men who were not only willing but able to shoot to kill.

Every war abounds with instances of superhuman individual exploits. Achilles is the forerunner of the type, which also includes Coriolanus (of Shakespeare's play of that name), Roland (of the *Song of Roland*), and El Cid. Although based, however slightly, on real people, these are all essentially literary characters. Yet some wars do produce instances of real-life counterparts—men who fight like one-man demolition crews. This is something that Marshall and du Picq, without saying it explicitly, lead us to expect. When the vast majority of those engaged in battle are by nature reluctant to fire and not very good at it under pressure, a rare individual who remains immune to fear can emerge as a seemingly otherworldly force. Such a fighter was Alvin York, a Tennessee backwoodsman with a talent for hunting wild turkeys, who distinguished himself as an Achilles among mortals in the First World War. The bare outline of his story has been told many times but is hardly ever explained, and can't be fully understood without some appreciation of the lessons of Marshall and du Picq.

The Phenomenon of Sergeant York

Alvin York went off to World War I involuntarily. Something of a hell-raiser before finding his religious calling in his late twenties, York applied for conscientious objector status when he was drafted in 1918, but was turned down. He was a savvy backwoods hunter and a crack shot, a remarkable talent even among his countrymen who lived off the land. Although he may have objected to the war in principle, he would eventually shed his compunction about killing Germans. While serving in the Argonne offensive in 1918, York is reported to have killed 25 of them, captured 132, and neutralized 35 machine guns single-handedly in one day. When asked about his one-man rampage, York said, "It weren't no trouble for me to hit them big army targets. They were so much bigger than turkey heads." As for the shooting ability of his comrades, he remarked, "They missed everything but the sky."

S.L.A. Marshall had come across such characters in the Second World War:

> During the mass interview of one infantry company in the Central Pacific, the statements of all concerned made it evident that one of the sergeants had performed so conspicuously during two days of attacks that the progress of the company had pivoted largely around his individual exploits. His company commander said, "When the fighting started, he practically took the company away from me. He was leading and the men were obeying him."

York's exploit in the Argonne bears closer inspection, not because there is anything suspicious about it but because the numbers by themselves can lead to the mistaken idea that something superhuman had taken place, when the reality was all too human. Rather than diminishing it, knowing how York pulled off his feat makes it all the more impressive.

Alvin York served in the 328th Infantry Regiment of the U.S. Army's 82nd Division as a corporal during a massive drive launched in the fall of 1918 by the French Marshall Ferdinand Foch, the newly appointed commander in chief of the Allied forces. The object of the offensive was to take the city of Sedan, a major rail center. As part of Foch's larger plan, the American forces were assigned the task of penetrating the Argonne Forest, a key link in the German defense and a formidable barrier. A week before York's battalion went into action, the famed Lost Battalion, commanded by Major Charles Whittlesey, was cut off in the Argonne and surrounded. But Whittlesey refused to surrender, and his brave stand inspired General Pershing to launch an attack to his west in an attempt to draw off the German stranglehold. This attack would include York's 82nd, which consisted of a high percentage of untested men.

Opposing them were German regiments that had reached the limits of their endurance. The fittest among them had gradually been siphoned off to bolster up depleted units in higher-priority areas. Morale among the remaining troops was low, and desertions were becoming a problem. Yet these were veteran fighters who enjoyed the advantage of an entrenched position ringed with nests of machine guns.

York's Company G missed out on the first successful American action, the taking of a hill that led to a German retreat and freed up the Lost Battalion. For his five-day holdout in the face of intense enemy pressure, Major Whittlesey would receive the Congressional Medal of Honor. But the Lost Battalion would be overshadowed by what came next, as York's company set off in support of a wave launched into the German lines. Making their way through mortar and machine-gun fire, the men of Company G became pinned down by nests of machine guns on a wooded hillside. To relieve the pressure, their commander sent three squads, including York's, to try to work their way around the gun emplacements. They did, only to find themselves a mile behind enemy lines with no idea where the Germans were.

At the same time the opposing German battalion, commanded by Lieutenant Vollmer, was equally confused. While attempting to move to a new position, Vollmer became disoriented, and when Company G launched its attack from the front, he was barely able to rally his men into a line of defense and open fire. Scrambling to find more men, Vollmer rushed to the rear of his position and discovered about two dozen German reserves lounging at breakfast. Before he could get them to move, three American squads, including York, burst in upon them from the rear and ordered the Germans to surrender. Most of the Germans threw down their arms immediately, but one soldier fired on the Americans. York, having by now seen too many of his comrades killed by machine gunners, let go of the last of his conscientious objections and shot the man dead.

The rest of Vollmer's battalion, meanwhile, was occupied with the frontal assault of Company G. But some of the machine gunners noticed the commotion to their rear and brought their guns around to bear on the Americans. They opened fire, hitting nine of them. York was lucky. He had been standing near the prisoners and was protected by the gunners' fear of hitting their own men. Whatever reservations York may have harbored about killing had completely vanished. He had seen enough, and now went into action.

York crouched low and moved toward the emplacements, making sure he stayed between the prisoners and the machine gunners. Carrying an Enfield rifle and with a Colt .45 automatic pistol draped over one finger, he sat down, placing himself below the sweep of the mounted guns, and one by one started picking off any German heads he saw peeking over the sandbags. Amid machine-gun fire and shouts, York calmly fired off shot after shot, apparently without missing. A few Germans, knowing that York was using a rifle with a five-round clip, tried to rush him with bayonets, unaware that he had the Colt. With his pistol, York proceeded to pick them off one by one, starting with the rearmost and then working his way forward until he had shot all five, a trick he had learned from turkey hunting. He knew that if the first one fell the others would either scatter or drop down and look for cover. By shooting the last man first, York convinced the others he was missing, and they kept coming until he had eliminated them all.

Lieutenant Vollmer also fired at York, but couldn't hit him. Faced with an apparently indestructible killing machine, Vollmer decided that the only sensible thing to do was to surrender. Twenty of his men already lay dead, and York seemed incapable of missing. So Vollmer blew a whistle, and Germans began filing out of the woods. One tried to throw a grenade, but York shot him down instantly.

The Americans had now taken even more prisoners than before, and under Corporal York's command (his superiors had been either killed or wounded in the action), they faced the more difficult task of bringing in the prisoners. York seems to have been unfazed. Ordering his men to gather the American wounded, he lined the Germans up in double file, placed three Americans on each side and one at the rear of the column, and in this arrangement marched them off toward the front. Along they way they passed more machine gun emplacements, each of which surrendered before this strange parade of men coming up from their rear. Completely taken by surprise, they offered no resistance, except for one soldier whom York shot without hesitation. When he finally brought this procession to the American position, York had amassed a total of 132 prisoners and was given credit for killing 25 others. For his day's work he was awarded the Congressional Medal of Honor.

The Price of Battle Readiness

The simplest way to account for the feats performed by Alvin York is to place them outside the realm of the merely human. Hollywood, in the 1941 film version that cast Gary Cooper as York (and earned Cooper an Oscar for best actor), played up a connection between York and Daniel Boone. The legendary Boone hailed from the same neck of the woods as York, and it was as if Hollywood, in attempting to stir up patriotic pride as the United States prepared to enter the Second World War, asked itself the question: what would Boone have done to the Germans, or what would Gary Cooper have done, for that matter? The answer was obvious; they would have done just what York did. But more inquiring minds, at least in retrospect, were not satisfied. S.L.A. Marshall, for one, wanted to know what really took place in such actions, and what he discovered would quite unintentionally assure that there would be no more Sergeant Yorks.

After the Second World War, the United States Army took Marshall's conclusions about men under fire to heart, and initiated a new training regimen designed to increase the rate of fire. It worked. In the Korean War, the fire rate increased to fifty percent, and in Vietnam it reached as high as ninety percent. But there was a downside. The brutality and dehumanization of the training did break down taboos about killing, but it also led to an increase in psychological casualties afterward. Unlike the Greek phalanx of ancient times, the new tactics required that each soldier shed all inhibitions about taking another man's life. No longer could the frontline soldier contribute simply by remaining in the ranks.

The effects of combat experience in Vietnam are complex and are still the object of intense debate. Many stereotypes of the Vietnam veteran have clouded the picture, but the literature suggests that battle readiness is a zero-sum game, in which reducing the taboo on killing increases psychological isolation. Some characters, like Alvin York, seem capable of compartmentalizing the task at hand without any dehumanizing training. York was one of the few, if not the only one on that battlefield that day, who not only had no reservations about shooting to kill, but was a deadly accurate shot even while under fire. In that respect his story is as much a paean to chance as to heroism. No such heroics would have occurred if there had been a

York in the German ranks that day, nor could they have occurred if the men on both sides had conformed to the stereotypes that Hollywood has created. In other words, York's brand of heroics would be unlikely to happen today because of changes in military training, if not in weaponry.

In the final analysis, Alvin York's rather human and somewhat accidental heroism is more reassuring than the usual monotonous recitation of tall tales—all action and no explanation. The crowning detail, usually omitted, is that "fire at will" is the most ironic of orders and, if strictly obeyed, would have brought most wars to a swift and grinding halt.

Put your trust in God, and fire at their shoelaces.

Oliver Cromwell
Battle of Marston Moor (English Civil War)
2 July 1644

Fire low.

Oliver Cromwell
Battle of Preston (English Civil War)
17 August 1648

*By push of bayonets—no firing till you see the whites
of their eyes.*

Frederick the Great
Battle of Prague
2 September 1744

*Men, you are all marksmen—don't one of you fire
until you see the whites of their eyes!*

General Israel Putnam
Battle of Bunker Hill
17 June 1775
Also attributed to William Prescott at the same battle.

Boys, aim at their waistbands.

Colonel John Stark
At the Battle of Bunker Hill
17 June 1775

*My opinion is that there ought not to be much firing
at all. My idea is that the best mode of fighting is to
reserve your fire till the army get—or you get them—
to close quarters. Then deliver one deadly, deliberate
volley—and charge!*

Stonewall Jackson
Rules of War

A French regiment opens fire on the English at the Battle of Neerwinden in 1692.

CHAPTER FOUR

Don't Fire until You See the Whites of Their Eyes!

In Search of the Perfect Volley at Fontenoy and Quebec

Ready, Level, Fire!

In a regimental historian's hands, a typical skirmish of the pre-Napoleonic era might go like something like this: Two formations of infantry, perhaps two or three ranks deep, march to within 30 paces of each other. Coolly and calmly they present their muskets. As the commander shouts out the order, "Ready, aim, fire!," the entire front rank, comprising hundreds or even thousands of men, simultaneously lets loose a volley from a range of deadly accuracy, with the result that the opposing front rank is mown down like wheat before a scythe.

What is wrong with this picture? To fans of hyperbolic battle tales it sounds like ripping stuff, a bloody good show. But if the testimony of the survivors is taken seriously, to get at anything even remotely close to the truth we would have to eliminate the words "coolly and calmly," as well as "entire" and "simultaneously," throw out the hackneyed allusion to harvesting, and give up any conceits about "deadly accuracy." Contrary to popular belief, infantrymen were almost never instructed to take aim. If anything, they were told to "level" their guns, which was about the best that could be hoped for.

This is bound to disappoint those who demand battles in which everyone fights bravely and shoots true. Some men, like Sergeant York, did. But most, as Charles Ardant du Picq and

S.L.A. Marshall discovered, were more recognizably human than that. If they shot their weapons at all, not only did they *not* shoot to kill, even to save their own lives, but they *could not* shoot, as the expression goes, to save their own lives.

One of the more astonishing aspects of Alvin York's feat is not his own uncanny shooting skill, but the inability of those around him to hit anything. Why, for example, did five Germans rush York with bayonets? Why didn't they simply shoot him? The answer, of course, is that the ability to shoot other human beings, especially when they are shooting back, is not as simple as it might appear on the silver screen. Some men may be willing to shoot, and some may be able to do it well, but it seems that the combination of the two in one person is rare.

That a talent like York's was exceptional was a fact well known to infantry commanders. Prince Hohenlohe, a Prussian commander of the Napoleonic era, conceded that "it is proof of superior military instruction if in battle the men only bring their rifles up to their shoulder and fire." Infantrymen were so notoriously inaccurate that few commanders attached any importance to aiming. Not only did the word *aim* rarely turn up in any battle order, but one Prussian officer went so far as to ban it, instructing his soldiers instead merely "to hold the rifle horizontally while keeping the head erect." In fact if accuracy and rapidity of fire were all that mattered, Napoleon would have outfitted his men with longbows.

Yet while less efficient as a destructive tool than the simpler weapons that preceded it, the gun had one overwhelming advantage—the frightening noise it made. In a world in which the threat of force counted for more than the application of it, gunpowder became the threat of choice long before anyone discovered how to do any real damage with it. Even when the unreliable arquebus evolved into the dependable Brown Bess musket, the gun remained highly ineffective for killing, not because it was inaccurate or difficult to use but because an amazingly high percentage of men armed with guns never made any attempt to shoot anyone with them. As the saying goes, guns don't kill, people do; and what amazed du Picq was just how few soldiers would willingly shoot to kill.

This, of course, hardly jibes with a popular stereotype that continues to be perpetuated well beyond its usefulness. But because no country still pins its hopes for military security on the myth of regimental firepower, the truth can now be told: infantry fire has always been erratic; its efficiency peaked in the eighteenth century and has declined ever since. The evidence can be found in regimental histories. Consider, for example, a celebrated incident from the Battle of Fontenoy, as famously related by Voltaire in his *History of the War of 1741*. Its notoriety rests upon a common assumption that is easily disproved.

The Battle of Fontenoy

On May 11, 1745, in one of many untidy clashes that punctuated the War of the Austrian Succession, several regiments of English Guards and Royal Scots marched to within 50 paces of a line of French infantry a few miles outside the Flemish village of Fontenoy. As the troops halted to dress ranks, Lord Charles Hay, the English captain, initiated a sporting challenge by calling out, "Gentlemen of the French Guards, open fire." A no less sporting reply came back from the Count d'Auteroche, a lieutenant of the French grenadiers: "Gentlemen, we never fire first; fire yourselves!" Having dispensed with these gallantries, Voltaire goes on to say, the English loosed a rolling volley.

This is the extent of the anecdote as it is usually extracted from Voltaire's lengthy account of the war. Certainly it is a marvelous story. But was chivalry the point, or was something else going on? At the risk of spoiling the story, we have to ask the obvious question: was there, against all common sense, a tactical advantage to offering the first shot to your adversary?

It turns out that in the era of linear formations, when one line of riflemen faced off against another, it was indeed wiser to let the other side fire first. Why? Not because it was good etiquette, but because it did indeed make perfectly good sense. Conditioned as we are to think of the regimental soldier as a cog in a well-oiled machine, we entirely discount the terror of his predicament. That is, we tend to overlook the emotional side of it. The regimental showdown resembled a duel, another instance in which it is better to let your opponent fire first. Commanders knew that a volley fired first under such pressure would for the most part miss its target, leaving the shooters vulnerable to a more accurate return volley or possibly a bayonet attack during the half a minute it took them to reload. Fear and the attendant inability to fire accurately (or at all) account for the ineffectiveness of the initial volley. Relief among the survivors, along with the knowledge that their opponent is momentarily disarmed while reloading, combine to produce a more effective return volley.

Yet the incident at Fontenoy seems to be an exception. Voltaire insists that the French, with the requisite sangfroid, induced the English to fire first, and yet they were immediately decimated. About 250 French were killed and 650 wounded. Their three remaining battalions dispersed without firing. It is only natural to ask what went wrong.

Part of the problem is missing information. Another version of the same battle, taken from J.W. Fortesque's *History of the British Army* (not exactly an unbiased source), supplies the critical details. Although usually omitted whenever Voltaire's charming anecdote is passed along, what brought the British to within 50 paces of the French is not irrelevant. The Redcoats could not have been in a very generous mood, having just survived a harrowing march through half a mile of open field bordered on two sides by French artillery redoubts that subjected them to deadly and continuous artillery fire. Many of the Redcoats fell, but others immediately filled the holes in the line. All this time the British resolutely withheld their own fire. When they finally reached a crest and drew up in impressive formation across from a startled and unprepared French infantry, they still held their fire. The action then focused on the commanders on either side. According to Fortesque:

> Lord Charles Hay of the First Guards stepped forward with a flask in hand, and doffing his hat drank politely to his enemies. "I hope, gentlemen," he shouted, "that you are going to wait for us today and not swim the Scheldt as you swam the Main at Dettingen. Men of the King's company," he continued, turning around to his own people, "these are the French Guards, and I hope you are going to beat them today"; and the English Guards answered with a cheer. The French officers hurried to the front, for the appearance of the British was a surprise to them, and called for a cheer in reply, but only a halfhearted murmur came from the French ranks, which quickly died away and gave place to a few sharp words of command; for the British were now within thirty yards. "For what we are about to receive may the Lord make us truly thankful," murmured an English Guardsman as he looked down the barrels of the French muskets, but before his comrades round him had done laughing the French Guards had fired; and the turn of the British had come at last.

In a footnote, Fortesque points out that every English account of the incident agrees: the French fired first. Given the outcome, this is believable. Not only were the French surprised by the arrival of the English, but they were disorganized and dispirited. In their confused state they made the mistake of firing a hasty and poorly executed volley, and of firing first. The more disciplined British, having withstood the terror of a long approach under artillery fire as well as the initial scattered volley, then vented all of their pent-up tension and suppressed fear on the dazed Frenchmen. Here is Fortesque, again with the requisite bluster and bravado, on what happened next:

For despite that deadly march through the crossfire of the French batteries to the muzzles of the French muskets, the scarlet ranks still glared unbroken through the smoke; and now the British muskets, so long shouldered, were leveled, and with crash upon crash the volleys rang out from end to end of the line . . . two battalions loading while the third fired, a ceaseless, rolling, infernal fire. Down dropped the whole of the French front rank, blue coats, red coats and white, before the storm. Nineteen officers and six hundred men of the French and Swiss Guards fell at the first discharge. . . . The British infantry were perfectly in hand; their officers could be seen coolly tapping the muskets of the men with their canes so that every discharge might be low and deadly; while the battalion-guns also poured in round after round of grape with terrible effect. The first French line was utterly shattered and broken.

Of course it is not that simple. Without having seen or participated in anything like it, a claim that none of us can make, we cannot easily imagine two lines of armed men some thirty yards apart, standing not only to fire, but to absorb volleys of musket fire. Nor can Voltaire or Fortesque. They rely on recollections that are too neat and clean, and thus create an intriguing but essentially false picture. For example, if we accept Fortesque's assertion that the British infantry fired with perfect composure from within a range of deadly accuracy, how could they have hit less than a tenth of the French? And why did their officers have to tap down the muskets to level the fire? We can only conclude that the average soldier aimed badly if he aimed at all, and that the damage inflicted owed mostly to the sheer volume of continuous firing, if not the grapeshot from the artillery (which sneaks almost unnoticed into the very end of Fortesque's description). The entire front rank did not drop down at once, nor did 600 men succumb to the first volley. The rest were not broken and scattered by the physical damage inflicted by British volley fire, but more likely by the noise of it, the surprise of it, and the dismay at their own ineffective volley. The artillery probably had even more to do with the result.

Unless we assume this, battle descriptions like the one below, courtesy of Marshal de Saxe, make no sense. (De Saxe, by the way, was the commander in chief of the French and Swiss forces at Fontenoy, who overcame the setback at the hands of the English Guards to win the battle.)

> At the battle of Castiglione [in 1796], the imperial troops let the French approach to twenty paces, hoping to destroy them by a volley. At that distance they fired coolly and with all precaution, but they were broken before the smoke cleared. At the battle of Belgrade (1717) I saw two battalions who at thirty paces aimed and fired at a mass of Turks. The Turks cut them up. . .

These two examples, which du Picq quotes in *Battle Studies*, at first sound authoritative; but they beg for explanation. How were the French "broken," and why? How could the Turks "cut up" two battalions that had just delivered a short-range volley? Du Picq quickly dispenses with such notions as firing "coolly and with all precaution." Unique among military analysts of the era for his acknowledgment of fear as a prime factor in war, du Picq dared to admit what most officers knew all too well: that terror and the emotions it draws forth dominate everything else on the battlefield and detract from the performance of troops. "The soldiers themselves have emotion," he wrote, "[and] their emotion never allows them to sight, or more than approximately adjust their fire. Often they fire into the air." To explain what probably happened at Castiglione and Belgrade, if not at Fontenoy, du Picq reaches for colorful metaphors:

> To make these men await, without firing, an enemy at twenty or thirty paces, needed great moral pressure. Controlled by discipline they waited, but as one waits for the roof to fall, for a bomb to explode. . . . When

the order is given to raise the arms and fire the crisis is reached. The roof falls, the bomb explodes, one flinches and the bullets are fired into the air. If anybody is killed it is an accident.

The obvious point is that if any infantry volley had been delivered with cool and murderous efficiency, the opposing front rank would indeed have been all but destroyed. While historians like to imagine such outcomes, there is no evidence to suggest it has ever happened. Something *like it* is supposed to have happened 14 years after Fontenoy at the Battle of Quebec, but here too a close reading is essential.

The Battle of Quebec

During the summer of 1759, near the end of the struggle for control of North America known as the French and Indian War, the British army under the command of General James Wolfe besieged the well-situated and highly fortified city of Quebec for two months. Repeated attempts by the British to reach the heights of the city by land and water had failed, until Wolfe got lucky. A scouting party discovered a narrow path that led up to the Plains of Abraham, which afforded the long-sought access to the walls of the city. On the night of the 12th of September, 4000 British soldiers made their way up this path, and on the following morning Wolfe mustered them on the Plains. They now stood poised to storm the city, and the French defenders had to move quickly to intercept them.

The battle unfolded more or less like Fontenoy, but with no artillery. Wolfe drew up his line of British Redcoats and ordered them to stand silent as the Marquis de Montcalm emerged with his troops from the city gate and advanced to intercept them. "The Battalion is not to halloo, or cry out, upon any account whatsoever," Wolfe told his men, "till they are ordered to charge with their bayonets." He had drilled this plan of battle into his troops to the point of tedium. "There is no necessity for firing very fast," he was given to say, "as a cool, well-leveled fire, with pieces carefully loaded, is much more destructive and formidable than the quickest fire in confusion." Wolfe understood the principles of regimental warfare very well, and he insisted upon waiting until the enemy advanced to within something close to whites-of-their-eyes range. Otherwise, he knew, his men would simply waste their ammunition. His Sergeant Major at Quebec recalled later that he gave "express orders not to fire until they came within twenty yards of us."

The fighting began when the French advanced in loosely formed columns and Montcalm sent sharpshooters out on the flanks with orders to maintain a harassing fire. Wolfe sent out skirmishers of his own to engage the sharpshooters and ordered the rest of his men in the ranks to lie face down. Meanwhile the French center advanced in three columns, and at a distance of about 200 yards began firing at will, while Wolfe's men remained down and did not return the fire. Only when the French drew to within 100 yards did Wolfe order his men to stand, to advance very deliberately, and still to withhold their fire.

If it did occur this way, it must have been a daunting sight to the French. At the same time, the tension in the British line must have been unbearable. Wolfe apparently sensed this because at 40 yards (instead of his preferred 20), his men let loose "with one deafening crash"—in the words, once again, of the honorable J. W. Fortesque. "The most perfect volley ever fired on a battlefield burst forth as if from a single monstrous weapon, from end to end of the British line." Amid the smoke, the British reloaded and fired again. When they advanced with bayonets, the French line broke and ran. Fortesque admiringly notes, "There was hardly a bullet of that volley that had not struck home."

While it is difficult to accept du Picq's contention that "if anybody is killed, it is an accident," it is just as hard to accept Fortesque's boastful claim. The truth must lie somewhere in between (but certainly closer to du Picq's estimation). It may well have been one of the deadliest volleys of all time, but the statistics are not so impressive. A well-drilled formation of British regulars, numbering (by historian Francis Parkman's estimate) about 3300, fired several volleys into a slightly larger French force (probably larger than 4000). The number of casualties (again rough estimates, in which the wounded far outnumber the dead) amounted to about 650 British and 1400 French. Assuming that each British soldier got off four shots during fifteen minutes of volley fire (which can only be taken as a conservative average, and a very rough one at that), no more than one in ten shots fired hit anyone. At best, we can safely say that the vast majority of shots hit nothing.

But a few did hit home. In the action both commanders, Montcalm of the French and Wolfe of the British, were mortally wounded. On the British side the event was chronicled in one of the most famous of all history paintings, Benjamin West's *Death of Wolfe*, a canvas whose rhapsodic pitch is tuned to the level of Fortesque's gushing prose. Because both Fortesque and Parkman shaped their accounts of the battle, if not the entire French and Indian War, to culminate in this single, thunderous burst of gunfire that brought down the heroic commanders on both sides, it is not surprising that both of their accounts are so unreliable. The event could not have been as simple as they describe it.

The Effectiveness of Volley Fire

What beat the French at Quebec? Some historians credit the victory to better training on the part of the British. Certainly the British showed better discipline, and this discipline of fire (rather than accuracy of fire) tipped the balance. Wolfe's insistence on drill, his sometimes brutal discipline, and his ability to withhold fire until the men were within whites-of-their-eyes distance allowed the British to achieve a more concentrated volume of fire, which unnerved the French and drove them from the field. The bayonet charge added the coup de grace and may well have been more effective than the volley. It is a telling point that the French did not run until the British advanced with bayonets.

This imbalance of discipline and morale accounts for almost all infantry victories. The day was won not by the physical damage inflicted by "the most perfect volley ever fired," but by what most nineteenth-century military analysts referred to as "moral force," an intangible quality that du Picq credits with making the difference in the Crimean War:

> It has been set down that the Russians were beaten at Inkerman by the range and accuracy of weapons of the French troops. But the battle was fought in thickets and wooded country, in a dense fog. . . . In either case, there could have been no accurate fire. The facts are that the Russians were beaten by superior morale; that unaimed fire, at random, . . . had the only material effect.

The material effect of rifle fire in regimental skirmishes has always been small. Even in the American Civil War, according to Paddy Griffith in his *Battle Tactics of the Civil War*, "musketry did not . . . possess the power to kill large numbers of men, even in very dense formations, at long range. At short range it could and did kill large numbers, but not very quickly." By "not very quickly" Griffith means that in the Napoleonic and American Civil Wars the casualty rate amounted to only *one or two men per minute*. Artillery inflicted proportionately more damage than small arms fire. As for the distressing number of deaths, Griffith explains, "casualties mounted because the contest went on so long, not because the fire was particularly deadly." This explains how regiments could and did hold positions, even in the open, for several hours under heavy fire.

This was not quite the situation at Fontenoy or Quebec. In both cases, the British used volley fire ("fire on command"), as opposed to skirmish fire ("fire at will"), against an enemy that stood fully exposed in a tight formation. Their fire was deadly, but not devastating. Even "the most perfect volley ever fired on a battlefield" resulted in no more than one hit in ten shots, a ratio that would never again be matched. As armies grew larger and rifles more accurate, the shots-to-hits ratio plummeted. In the Franco-German War of 1870, it stood at about one hit in 200 shots. Time and again in modern battles, participants marveled at how little damage could result from so much firing. One medic in Vietnam noted, "One of the things that amazed me is how many bullets can be fired during a firefight without anyone getting hurt."

Most accounts of battles and skirmishes not involving artillery fire, including massacres, tend to bear this out. It is not unusual to read of an incident in which a great number of men fire away with abandon, often at very close range, only to discover that the number of casualties barely rose above single digits. One witness to a nighttime firefight at Vicksburg in 1863 remarked, "It seems strange . . . that a company of men can fire volley after volley at a like number of men at not over a distance of fifteen steps and not cause a single casualty. Yet such was the facts in this instance."

Another good example was provided by the men of Major Marcus Reno's three companies at Little Big Horn. They were the lucky ones who attacked the Lakotas from the south while Custer rode off with his five companies to attack the Indian camp from the east. Both detachments were outnumbered by their opponents, but Reno's 200 men fared better than Custer's. The terrain provided some cover, and the Indians he encountered were surprised and disorganized. In his book *Custer and the Epic of Defeat*, Bruce Rosenberg summarized the action this way:

> Sergeant Ryan thought that the enemy numbered 500; Reno himself put the figure at 800 to 1000. The hostiles swarmed his left flank and the firing was intense. Yet in the first thirty minutes or so, Reno suffered only three casualties, and two of them because the soldiers' horses bolted into Indian "lines." A thousand men

banging, and whizzing, and clubbing away, and only three men hit!

But is this really so surprising? The natives appear to have been, at first, reluctant fighters. Although described as savages brought up from childhood to fight, this was merely a convenient stereotype. They were not much different from their adversaries when it came to killing. Many members of the Seventh Cavalry had never fired a gun in anger, and the same was true of the Indians. From their accounts of the battle we know that each chief had to work desperately to rally his braves and convince them to fight. Chief Two Moon, who led his men against Reno, gave this testimony:

> I got on my horse and rode out into my camp. I called out to the people all running about: "I am Two Moon, your chief. Don't run away. Stay here and fight. You must stay and fight the white soldiers. I shall stay even if I am to be killed."

On the Cavalry side, Lieutenant Charles A. Varnum had this to say:

> When the skirmish line was formed I saw a good many excited men shooting right up in the air . . . Reynolds was very anxious to get a drink of whiskey out of his flask, and to tell the truth, I was paying more attention to that than I was to the Indians.

Such candid remarks are usually edited out of the legends because of the unflattering light they shine on both sides. Under heavy fire from mounted braves using Winchester repeating carbine rifles, Reno's company fired back just as ineffectively with their single-shot Springfields. As the Lakotas who witnessed Custer's last stand succinctly put it, "They did not seem to know how to shoot."

Not many infantrymen did. In the eighteenth century the British army's Brown Bess tested accurate to within 6 inches at

40 yards, which is about the distance at which the whites of the eyes become evident. At 100 yards, accuracy fell off considerably: the most skilled marksmen could hit a two-foot by two-foot target only half the time. But such tests took for granted two things that are in short supply in battle—skilled shooters and the composure necessary for aiming. Du Picq was more realistic:

> Look at these two ranks crouched under the cover of a small trench. Follow the trajectory of the shots. Even note the trajectory shown by the burst of flame. You will be convinced that, under such circumstances, even simple horizontal fire is a fiction. In a second, there will be wild firing on account of the noise, the crowding, the interference of the two ranks. Next everybody tries to get under the best possible cover. Good-bye firing.

The Fastest with the Mostest

Little wonder, then, that "Don't fire until you see the whites of their eyes" is such a well-known battle order. It has been attributed to Prince Charles of Prussia at Jagendorf in 1745, to Frederick the Great at Prague in 1757, and to both of the opposing commanders at the Battle of Bunker Hill in 1775. The idea is simple and practical. It says nothing about aiming and everything about timing. Fire as a unit, not precisely at the same instant, but almost. Fire when your enemy is not too far away, but not so close that he can get to you before you can reload. And don't fire first.

The desired musket range at Fontenoy, Quebec, and Bunker Hill was about 40 yards, a distance the enemy could cover in about 30 seconds, or about the time it took to reload. In other words, it was a critical distance for that type of weapon—close enough for accuracy, far enough for safety from bayonets.

What Fontenoy and Quebec prove is that even whites-of-their-eyes shooting, if it was not very accurate, could still be effective. The point was to induce the enemy to break off by intimidating them. It was the volume of fire that won battles, not the accuracy. Only by the application of force through constant firing did troops manage to maintain their position or move forward. Frederick the Great, a military aphorist second only to Napoleon, acknowledged as much when he remarked that firing was simply a means to "quiet and occupy undependable soldiers." In a less flippant mood, he might have seconded Colonel Nathan Bedford Forrest's personal philosophy of getting there "the fastest with the mostest." The goal was not to kill more of the enemy, but to break their morale and thereby break their ranks. That is how gunfire managed to be effective without being deadly.

The only means we have of confirming any of this today is by frequenting reenactments, particularly those of Civil War battles, in which the number of participants occasionally approximates (if only locally) the real thing. In their quest for historical accuracy, most reenactors border on the fanatical. But one of the most authentic aspects of their performances is instinctual rather than planned. Even though their weapons are not firing real Minié balls, most of the reenactors aim and fire high. Again, as du Picq noted, "if anybody is killed, it is an accident."

Fix bayonets! Charge bayonets, charge!

Col. Joshua Chamberlain
At Little Round Top
Battle of Gettysburg
2 July 1863

Come on! Come on, boy!

Lieutenant W. S. Melcher
At the same battle

Come on, my lads, who will follow me?

Sir Charles Russell
Battle of Inkerman (Crimean War)
5 November 1854

Fix bayonets, charge, and keep up the hill.

Assistant Surgeon Wolseley
At Inkerman

Every man who loves this flag, follow me!

A French colonel
At Solferino
Italian Wars of Independence
24 June 1859

Leading the charge up Henry House Hill at the first Battle of Bull Run, July 1861. From a drawing by Walter Taber for Battles and Leaders of the Civil War.

CHAPTER FIVE

Come on, Lads! Who Will Follow Me?

LITTLE ROUND TOP AND OTHER LOCAL SITUATIONS

Points of View

For many history buffs, the Battle of Gettysburg epitomizes the entire Civil War. If it had to be boiled down even further, the entire conflict could be encapsulated by the extraordinary struggle that took place during the second day of the battle on a hill called Little Round Top. It was there that the 20th Maine Volunteers fended off the 15th Alabama Regiment, repulsing them with a bayonet charge over ground that, as Shelby Foote has noted, lies at the precise geographical midpoint between the hometowns of the men on either side. Aficionados of the game of "what might have been" are moved by such coincidences to isolate this one incident and use it to chart the probable course of history if this or that had or had not happened. What if the Maine volunteers had folded? What if the Alabamians had had just 20 more men? Such hypothetical questions then escalate into assertions of the importance of one thing over another, to the point that a single skirmish can emerge as the single most decisive moment in an entire nation's history. Such is the enthusiasm that the men who fought on Little Round Top unintentionally inspired.

For our purposes, however, Little Round Top is simply a good example of a local action in which very human qualities were on display. Many of those who fought were brave; some were not. Some physically able men did not participate in the fighting. On the whole, the accuracy of fire was poor. The commanders ordered charges and countercharges, in which success or failure hinged on the actions of a few men. The day was won not by gunfire, but by a bayonet charge.

What most writers tend to overlook, carried away as they are by the symbolic potential of the moment, is that the men who fought there had no interest in epitomizing the entire war. Once under fire, they had little use for political, religious, or moral slogans or any of the altruistic motives that brought them to that spot. What sustained them once the firing began was something far more immediate.

During the Hundred Years' War of the fourteenth and fifteenth centuries, the English fought for God and St. George and the French fought for St. Denis, if we can believe their battle cries. Before the fighting began, fighting words undoubtedly meant something to those soldiers. The lore of battle is sprinkled with too many such phrases to deny their importance, at least before battle. But when push came to shove and shove came to shot, St. George stepped aside as men fought for each other—for the men on the right and the left. This is what the memoirs tell us. Having no idea of the scale or importance of what they were caught up in, men in a fight responded to what they could see and hear, and God, St. George, St. Denis, and the rest of the world could go to hell. This is the essence of what some writers (notably S.L.A. Marshall) refer to as the local situation.

Why Battles Look More Realistic at the Cinema

In *The Ebb and Flow of Battle*, R. J. Campbell, a World War I gunner, wrote, "You don't see very much of a battle when you are taking part in it. In March [1918] I had seen lines of German infantry coming downhill at a run, now I saw tanks going up a hill and our men walking quite slowly behind them. That was all I saw of two battles. It's much better on TV or at the cinema, the battles there look far more realistic."

It does look more realistic at the cinema, but that is because of our confusion about what is real in battle. Napoleon claimed that "the only thing my Grenadiers saw of Russia was the pack on the man in front." Of course, they also saw the battles, but how much of them did they really see? In *Men Against Fire*, S.L.A. Marshall summed up battle from the point of view of the fighting man when he wrote:

> In battle you may draw a small circle around a soldier, including within it only those persons or objects which he sees or which he believes will influence his immediate fortunes. These primarily will determine whether he rallies or fails, advances or falls back.
>
> Unconsciously, perhaps, we have recognized this truth. The noblest phrases in our whole military tradition pay tribute to the overpowering impact of the local situation upon the spirit and will of the fighting man.
>
> "Don't give up the ship!"
>
> "Don't fire until you see the whites of their eyes!"
>
> "I think it would be better to order up some artillery and defend the present location." . . . The words of U.S. Grant during the Battle of the Wilderness.
>
> "To hell with our artillery mission. We've got to be infantrymen now." . . . The words of Lt. Col. Thornton L. Mullins at Omaha Beachhead.

But we've been conditioned to recognize a different truth. History books, films, and television show us battles from a bird's-eye perspective. Consequently, inspiring phrases like those quoted by Marshall come off not as being from one small incident in a great battle, but as being the essence of the entire battle, if not the war. The reality is that if they were spoken at all, they were only heard by a few men in the immediate vicinity. Once sprung loose from that limited context, however, they echo throughout the theater of war, creating the illusion of a large-scale team effort. This is one of the ways that war provides a grand stage for writers, painters, and movie directors. But for those who actually fight, the experience is quite different. Questioned about it afterwards, they commonly remark how *unlike* the movies it is, and how limited their own view of it was. Marshall rightly believed that only by appreciating a hundred "local situations" could we begin to appreciate the big picture. Unfortunately, many historians insist upon cutting to the chase by using an isolated incident to represent the entire battle, usually resulting in the diminishment of both. Which brings us back to Little Round Top.

The Struggle for Little Round Top

On the second day of the Battle of Gettysburg, the Union army commanded by General Meade held a front dominated on the left by a small hill known as Little Round Top. Being bare of trees, this hill afforded a 360-degree view of the battlefield and would, if taken by the enemy and fortified with artillery, have made the position of the Union army untenable. But Meade dismissed its significance, assuming that the Confederates would concentrate their attack elsewhere. Consequently, he paid little attention to his far left, which is how it eventually came to be defended by an untested volunteer regiment commanded by a college professor.

At the same time, the Confederates under Lee did more or less what Meade had expected, at least until General Hood, commanding the division on the Confederate right, requested permission to take his men even further to the right in an attempt to turn the Union flank. The request was denied, but as the advance unfolded, Hood's far right became tangled up: Two regiments, one of which was the 15th Alabama, began to cross paths. As a consequence, the Alabamians were ordered to proceed further to the right, into the valley between Little Round Top and the wooded peak of Big Round Top.

This was the big picture, and it explains how the Confederates managed to take Big Round Top, which was defended only by a company of sharpshooters, and why William C. Oates, the commander of the 15th Alabama, would naturally proceed to Little Round Top, which to him appeared undefended. What he could not have known was that a Union engineer who was reconnoitering the battlefield at the same time also noticed the vulnerability of Little Round Top. Because of the engineer's alertness, Union commanders decided to send the nearest available unit, Joshua Chamberlain and his 20th Maine Volunteers, racing to the hill. They arrived just in time—15 minutes ahead of Oates—and thus set the stage for one of the most memorable showdowns of the war.

Chamberlain, a professor at Bowdoin College, led a group of untested Maine farmers who were eager to prove themselves but had no idea what they were walking into. Oates, on the other hand, led an experienced bunch, but he had lost a few dozen of them before reaching Little Round Top. In addition, he had just sent 20 men to fill the canteens, and they would not return. Thus on a hot summer day, having marched more than 30 miles the day before, the Alabamians faced an uphill battle without any water, against an entrenched company of about the same size. The two forces fought fiercely, each sustaining heavy casualties. Chamberlain described it this way:

> Squads of the enemy broke through our line in several places, and the fight was literally hand to hand. The edge of the fight rolled backward and forward like a wave. The dead and wounded were now in our front and then in our rear. Forced from our position, we desperately recovered it, and pushed the enemy down to the foot of the slope. The intervals of the struggle were seized to remove our wounded . . . to gather ammunition from the cartridge boxes of the disabled friend or foe on the field, and even to secure better muskets.

Chamberlain's men were fast running out of ammunition. The struggle had gone on for more than an hour when Oates regrouped his men for one more make-or-break charge. "The enemy seemed to have gathered all their energies for their final assault," wrote Chamberlain. "We had gotten our thin line into as good a shape as possible, when a strong force emerged from the scrub wood in the valley, as well as I could judge, in two lines in echelon by the right, and, opening a heavy fire, the first line came on as if they meant to sweep everything before them." But Chamberlain's line held, and the charge of the Alabamians faltered.

Descriptions of the battle at this point reach a crescendo of dire implications. The Maine regiment was just about out of ammunition. The Union regiments to their right were hard-pressed and unable to give support. It looked like the end. The Maine men knew what was at stake, as did their opponents from Alabama. Oates knew that he too had no help coming. The fate of the Union hung in the balance.

Much of this, of course, is debatable and endlessly debated. What is not at issue, however, is the logic of Chamberlain's decision to charge. His own men balked at first. When Chamberlain yelled out, "Fix bayonets! Charge bayonets, charge!" there must have been a moment of hesitation, because we are then told that Lieutenant H.S. Melcher stepped forward, drew his sword, and charged down the hill yelling, "Come on! Come on, boy!" The regiment followed, yelling and brandishing their bayonets.

In *Battle Studies*, Charles Ardant du Picq contended that only rarely would a battalion hold its ground before a bayonet charge. "No enemy awaits you if you are determined," he wrote, "and never, never, never, are two equal determinations opposed to each other." In those rare instances when one side did hold their ground before bayonets, it was only because each man froze with fear and failed to defend himself. According to du Picq, this explains the massacres of ancient battles. These thoughts have since been seconded by many other military theorists. Lieutenant Colonel David Grossman for one, in his book *On Killing*, reviews the literature on bayonet charges and concludes that "the average soldier has an intense resistance toward bayoneting his fellow man, and that this act is surpassed only by the resistance to *being* bayoneted." Consequently, "soldiers who would bravely face a hail of bullets will consistently flee before a determined individual with cold steel in his hands."

Here, then, is yet another myth that has been foisted on us by countless movies: the bayonet charge that culminates in a savage free-for-all of stabbing and slashing. According to the best evidence available, most of those bayoneted in battle were men who were too physically incapacitated to move, too mentally incapacitated to resist, or who turned and ran and were stabbed in the back. Little Round Top is just one of countless examples in which a bayonet charge succeeded with no actual bayoneting. The exhausted and dehydrated Alabamians had used up their reserves of determination. Having been repulsed again and again, they were completely unnerved by the charge. According to Chamberlain, who himself was just learning the lesson, "The effect was surprising . . . many of the enemy's first line threw down their arms and surrendered. . . . Holding fast by our right, and swinging forward with our left, we made an extended 'right wheel,' before which the enemy's second line broke and fell back, fighting tree to tree, many being captured, until we had swept the valley and cleared the front of nearly our entire brigade."

Oates would later insist that he had ordered a retreat, much like Ryzhov had in the face of the Highlanders at Balaclava. But whether such an order was given or not, he conceded that "we ran like a herd of wild cattle."

Who Will Follow Me?

In *Men Against Fire*, S.L.A. Marshall noted that in any crisis, "could one clear commanding voice be raised—even though it be the voice of an individual without titular authority—they would obey, or at least the stronger characters would do so, and the weaker would begin to take heart because something is being done." This, in Marshall's view, is not only the key to the local situation, but the key to all battles: someone must rise to the occasion and say a few clear and unambiguous words, telling the group what to do. Unfortunately, Marshall concedes, "clear, commanding voices are all too rare on the field of battle."

Marshall's criticism is directed primarily at Americans, whose soldiers, he believed, tended to shy away from speech, and thus often failed to achieve the level of teamwork that can only be brought about through talk. Just as coaches encourage their players to talk constantly in order to let their teammates know where they are and what they are doing, Marshall stressed the importance of words as a tactical necessity:

> Speech galvanizes the desire to work together. It is the beginning of the urge to get something done. Until there is speech, each soldier is apt to think of his situation in purely negative terms. With the coming of speech he begins to face up to it. . . . An excited lieutenant shouting: "Get the hell out of here and follow me to that tree line on the far side of the creek," will succeed . . . . Formal language under these circumstances is almost unknown in the Army of the United States. In fact, "Get the hell out of here!" has virtually established itself in our jargon as a customary order.

Admittedly, Marshall wrote about soldiers who fought in the Second World War, but his observations, judging by how well they fit the facts at Little Round Top, get at the essence of men in battle. He could have used Lieutenant Melcher to illustrate this point, or Sir Charles Russell, a British officer at the Battle of Inkerman in the Crimean War, who rose up before a group of Coldstream Guards that had lost its commander and said, "Come on, my lads, who will follow me?" Or assistant surgeon Wolseley, who in the same battle found himself the only officer in sight and rallied a squad of outnumbered Redcoats with the words, "Fix bayonets, charge, and keep up the hill." Or "Le Colonel de Maleville," a French colonel at the Battle of Solferino, who cried out, "Every man who loves this flag, follow me!"

We can safely assume that the language in these examples was cleaned up a bit. Marshall claimed that formal language is almost unknown in the heat of the local situation. When the bombs start flying no one takes the time to find just the right words. High ideals fall by the wayside. Commands had better be blunt and forceful, laced with obscenity when emphasis is required, and stripped of any nonsense. As for entertaining thoughts of God, of country, of family, of principles or ideals, the poet Robert Graves, in summing up his experiences in the trenches of the First World War, wrote, "Hardly one soldier in a hundred was inspired by religious feeling of even the crudest kind. It would have been difficult to remain religious in the trenches even if one survived the irreligion of the training at home." Nor, he contends, did politics enter into it. "The battalion cared as little about the successes and reverses of our Allies as about the origins of the war. It never allowed itself to have any political feelings about the Germans. A professional soldier's duty was simply to fight whomever the King ordered him to fight."

In fact, as Graves and other combat veterans attest, only two things matter to a soldier under fire: his regard for the men he serves with and his pride in his own regiment. Even then a soldier will tend to narrow that focus to men of his particular unit, and sometimes only those he can see and hear.

In *Goodbye Darkness*, his memoir of the war in the Pacific, William Manchester recalls an assault on one of many Japanese-held atolls. Pinned down at the base of a sea wall by machine-gun fire, Manchester and his squad had to suffer the gung-ho bravado of a replacement officer who wanted them to charge directly into the Japanese machine gunners, when a flanking maneuver was clearly called for. "Men, I know you'd like to stay here," the officer said. "I would myself. But those yellow bastards down the beach are killing your buddies." The buddies, in this case, were the men of the First Battalion, some 400 yards down the beach. But the appeal fell on deaf ears. "He didn't even realize that a combat man's loyalty is confined to those around him," comments Manchester, "that as far as [we] were concerned the First Battalion might as well have belonged to a separate race."

No one followed the replacement officer when he led the charge over the sea wall. They waited the half a second it took for him to be ripped apart by machine-gun fire, and then executed their flanking maneuver—successfully.

In other words, men in battle have little interest in the big picture, and focus only on the immediate objective. "Lofty ideals we must have," wrote Marshall, "if only to assure that man will go forward." But in the heat of such intense activity, men are not moved by thoughts of God and country, of glory and honor, of home and hearth. What we are only occasionally told is that the fighting man's greatest fear is of letting down his buddies, and that he fights as the ancient Greeks did, for the man on the left, the man on the right, and for himself.

Tales That Redound to the Glory of Our Arms

To be fair, historians do not always have the freedom to dwell on the local situation. When they survey the full course of events, they have to stick to describing causes, clashes, and consequences in broad terms. A truer picture of what war is like, according to Leo Tolstoy, is available only to the artist, by which he means the novelist. Tolstoy lays out the case for this contention in an epilogue to *War and Peace*, in which he explains that the Napoleonic Wars can best be described by examining the individual experiences of a wide range of participants, and that only the sum of such experiences can approximate the whole. "The historian has to deal with the results of an event," he notes, "the artist with the fact of the event."

The proof of Tolstoy's point is in the pudding, in his sprawling masterpiece that shows war as unlike anything we could have imagined, because it is unlike anything his own characters were able to imagine. Here, for example, Nicholas Rostov, a young hussar hardened by bitter experience, reacts to a war story as one who now knows better, as one who cannot see battle as anything but a confused mass of local situations:

Zdrzhinsky . . . spoke grandiloquently of the Saltanov dam being a "Russian Thermopylae," and of how a deed worthy of antiquity had been performed by General Raevsky. He recounted how Raevsky had led his two sons onto the dam under terrific fire, and had charged with them beside him. Rostov heard the story and not only said nothing to encourage Zdrzhinsky's enthusiasm, but on the contrary looked like a man ashamed of what he was hearing, though with no intention of contradicting it. . . . Rostov knew by experience that men always lie when describing exploits, as he himself had done when recounting them; besides that, he had experienced enough to know that nothing happens in war at all as we can imagine or relate it. And so he did not like Zdrzhinsky's tale. . . . "In the first place, there must have been such a confusion and crowding on the dam that was being attacked, that if Raevsky did lead his sons there it could have no effect except perhaps on some dozen men nearest to him," thought he, "the rest could not have seen how or with whom Raevsky came onto the dam. And even those who did see it would not have been much stimulated by it, for what had they to do with Raevsky's tender paternal feelings when their own skins were in danger? And besides, the fate of the Fatherland did not depend on

85

whether they took the Saltanov dam or not, as we are told was the case at Thermopylae. So why should he have made such a sacrifice? And why expose his own children in the battle?" . . . Nicholas continued to think, as he listened to Zdrzhinsky. But he did not express his thoughts for in such matters, too, he had gained experience. He knew that this tale redounded to the glory of our arms and so one had to pretend not to doubt it. And he acted accordingly.

Glory is the bending of reality to suit some ulterior purpose. It results from blowing a local situation out of proportion in order to serve as a moral lesson. This has its uses. But once those purposes are no longer pressing and we allow ourselves to cast a more critical eye on history, it is also useful to reassess any view of the past that strikes us as a gratuitous embellishment.

The struggle for Little Round Top, by virtue of its strategic importance, contributed far more to the Battle of Gettysburg than Raevsky's heroics did at Austerlitz. But there is always a Zdrzhinsky to whip the bare facts into a glorious froth and claim that this tiny fractal epitomizes the whole war. While we are under no obligation to adopt the skepticism of Nicholas Rostov, neither should we unquestioningly accept accounts of war that merely "redound to the glory of our arms." There is still much to admire in history told straight.

He who leaves a fight, loses it.
French proverb

*Any officer or soldier . . . who presumes to turn his back and
flee, shall instantly be shot down, and all good officers are
hereby authorized and required to see this done, that the
brave and gallant part of the Army shall not fall a sacrifice
to the base and cowardly part, or share their disgrace in a
cowardly and unmannerly retreat.*
George Washington
Letter to the President of Congress
20 September 1776

*Always mystify, mislead, and surprise the enemy, if possible;
and when you strike and overcome him, never give up the
pursuit as long as your men have strength to follow; for an
enemy routed, if hotly pursued, becomes panic-stricken, and
can be destroyed by half their number.*
Stonewall Jackson
Rules of War

*Be men now, dear friends, and take up the heart of courage
and have consideration for each other in the strong encounters,
since more come through alive when men consider each other,
and there is no glory when they give way, nor warcraft either.*
Agamemnon
To the Greeks
The *Iliad* of Homer, book V, line 529

*Far it be for us to do such a thing as flee from them. If our
time has come, let us die bravely for our brethren, and leave
no question of our honor.*
Judas Maccabias
1 Maccabees 9:10

Retreat, hell! We just got here.
Captain Lloyd S. Williams, USMC
Battle of Belleau Wood
3 May 1918

"Crossing the Beresina." Napoleon's Grande Armée retreats from Moscow in 1812. From a drawing by E. Bayard.

CHAPTER SIX

Sauve Qui Peut!

THE TRICKY BUSINESS OF RETREAT

Pandemonium

To most of us, the Greek god Pan is a creature with a man's body and arms, a goat's legs and tail, a horned head, and a talent for playing the pipes. To the Romantic painters and poets he was the god of mischievous love, a symbol of idyllic, rustic, and pastoral simplicity, and a patron of shepherds. But to the ancient Greeks, Pan's true talent lay not in love or in peace, but in war, where he was thought to be responsible for a great deal of mischief. If we choose to believe Herodotus, this seemingly carefree god played the heavy in the majority of battles ever fought, accounting for more deaths than any other single factor. His methods, well known to warriors of the past, constituted one of their greatest fears, leading every commander to hope that if Pan showed his face at all on the battlefield, it would be among the enemy.

From Pan we get *panic* and *pandemonium*, words that spell doom for an army. When the pipes of Pan induced a soldier to turn and flee from the field of battle, the effect could be wildly contagious and almost always disastrous. It must have been a common occurrence. In his account of the Peloponnesian War, the Greek historian Thucydides describes an encounter in which "the barbarians were instantly seized with one of those unaccountable panics to which great armies are liable." The fourth-century BC Greek military writer Aeneas (known as the Tactician), who lived through the invasions of Philip of Macedon, wrote a chapter on how to deal with "the confusions

89

and terrors that suddenly arise in a city or a camp, by night or by day, [and] are by some called *panics*—a word invented in the Peloponnese, more particularly in Arcadia." The reference, of course, is to Pan, who made his home in a mountainside cave in the Greek state of Arcadia.

In the modern era Pan's role remained essentially unchanged, but his pipes have been replaced by a few highly charged phrases that can and did have the same snowball effect when shouted in the wrong place or at the wrong time. The most notorious such expression is *"Sauve qui peut!"* Roughly translated, it means "Every man for himself," and in practice it signals the disintegration of an army, its almost certain defeat, and quite possibly its annihilation. Along with its equivalent, "Run for your lives," it can instigate a panic, which can turn into a rout, which can easily turn into a massacre.

It was only natural for the Athenians to assume that Pan ran amok among the invading Persians at the Battle of Marathon in 490 BC. How else to explain why the enemy fled from the field, allowing the Greeks to slaughter them and win a decisive victory? This is the battle, it should be recalled, that inspired the foot race of the same name. It was run for the first time by Philippides (or Pheidippides), a professional runner sent by the Athenians to seek help from Sparta.* On his way there Philippides passed through southeastern Arcadia, where he encountered Pan near his cave on Mount Parthenius. Given this unexpected opportunity, the god asked the messenger why the Athenians had been neglecting him recently, given the number of times he had helped them in the past. Although Philippides had no answer, he relayed Pan's question to his comrades, and after the battle they acknowledged the god's

---

*The distance from Athens to Sparta is 156 miles, which Herodotus says Philippides covered in a day, a feat which has been proven possible in modern re-creations. The Roman satirist Lucian, however, has Philippides not only run from Athens to Sparta, but back to the battle at Marathon, and from there to Athens, about 26 miles away, where he delivers the news of the victory and drops dead on the spot. The Athenians established a yearly torch race in his honor. The modern marathon, of course, mercifully uses the Marathon-to-Athens distance rather than the distance from Athens to Sparta.

good will by erecting a temple to Pan below the Acropolis and establishing a yearly festival in his honor.

The story is typical of the many colorful details Herodotus weaves into his history of the Persian wars. It links the historical fact of the headlong Persian retreat on the plain of Marathon to the fanciful myth of the intervention of Pan. Yet it also makes a larger point about the unpredictability of battle. No one could say in advance what might make either side run from a fight, but most battles were decided this way. When it happened it was usually so catastrophic that it appeared as if only the gods could have caused it.

Conquer or Die

Because battle histories tend to focus on commanders, it is all too easy to buy into an idea that every commander hoped everyone would believe—that the army was simply an extension of his own will, as responsive to his wishes as his own right hand. Frederick the Great wanted to believe it; Julius Caesar wrote as though he did believe it. But if this had truly been the case, they would have had no reason to fear a retreat.

In *Instructions to His Generals*, Frederick writes, "I make vows to Heaven that the Prussians never shall be obliged to make retreats." But his prayers were not answered. He himself had to swallow his pride and withdraw at the Battle of Kolin in 1757, after his right wing panicked and ran from the Austrians. And yet while Frederick may not have exercised as much control as he would have us believe, his opponents did believe it, which was what he counted on. Because premodern wars (meaning wars fought before the advent of the machine gun, the tank, and the airplane) often amounted to large-scale bluffing contests, it was crucial not only not to back down, but to make sure your enemy was convinced you would never even think of it. So important was this equation that the tone of an entire war was often set in the very first battle.

At the First Battle of Bull Run in the American Civil War, a well-conceived but poorly executed Union charge came up against Stonewall Jackson's division on Henry House Hill. The Confederates' ability to stand firm not only repulsed the charge but led to a panicked Union retreat all the way back to Washington. From then on, Union soldiers, much like Stephen Crane's Henry Fleming in *The Red Badge of Courage*, felt unsure of themselves and convinced of the superiority of the Confederate infantryman. What allowed this delusion to harden into a grim truth was the fact that after this one incident, the Confederates believed it too. When General Barnard E. Bee saw Jackson's men hold the line at Henry House Hill, he supposedly called out to his own men, "Look! There is Jackson, standing like a stone wall. Let us determine to die here, and we will conquer." This was not so much a command as a promise. Standing like a stone wall guaranteed the repulse of even the finest charge. It not only earned Jackson and his Stonewall Division their nicknames, but won for the entire Confederate army a reputation that would serve it well.

The tricky business of retreat partly explains why "conquer or die" is such a pervasive battle cry. Many armies have backed themselves into positions in which it was literally true. If they did not persevere and conquer, which is to say if they backed down, they would have been either wiped out or put on the defensive for the remainder of the war. According to the Bible's First Book of Kings, at the Battle of Ramothgilead in the ninth century BC, King Ahab of Israel disguised himself before going into battle, knowing that the king of Syria had given his men the order to "fight with neither small nor great, save only with the king of Israel." The Syrians knew that if Ahab fell, his army would crumble. By chance, at the height of the battle a Syrian archer's arrow lodged between the plates of Ahab's armor and pierced his chest. Unwilling to let his troops know the truth, which was that he was grievously wounded, and with the outcome of the battle still in doubt, the king kept to the field "and the blood ran out of the wound into the midst of the chariot." The day was saved but Ahab was not. News of his death so disheartened his men that they retreated, "every man to his city, and every man to his own country."

At the turning point of the Battle of Hastings in 1066, the Normans panicked, thinking that William the Conqueror had fallen. According to William's biographer, William of Poitiers, when the Norman king saw what was happening he rallied his men with threats of shame:

> Baring his head and lifting his helmet, he cried, "Look at me. I am alive, and with God's help I will conquer. What madness is persuading you to flee? What way is open to escape? You could slaughter like cattle the men who are pursuing and killing you. You are abandoning victory and imperishable fame, and hurrying to disaster and perpetual ignominy. Not one of you will escape death by flight." At these words they recovered their courage. He rushed forward at their head, brandishing his sword, and mowed down the hostile people who deserved death for rebelling against him, their king.

William of Poitiers is honest enough to admit that he has invented the dialogue, as if it were not obvious enough. The words are more appropriate to center stage than the midst of a melee. But they illustrate the relevant point, that the army's fortunes turned upon those of its commander. At Hastings this point was further driven home on the other side of the field when an arrow found its way through the eye slit in King Harold's helmet. Unlike Ahab, the Saxon king could not hide his wound. When he fell, his side was doomed.

Of course, not all generals have been quite so stalwart. At Gaugemela in 331 BC, Alexander the Great, leading fewer than 50,000 Macedonians, penetrated the ranks of a larger Persian force, inducing their leader, Darius III, to flee from the battlefield. A panic then ensued; someone must have shouted that all

93

was lost. The Macedonians chased down the fleeing Persians, slaughtering them over a distance of 50 miles. When the chase was finally called off, Darius' army had lost somewhere between 40,000 and 90,000 (estimates vary), as opposed to fewer than 500 for the Macedonians. The battle had been more or less equal to that point, and relatively low in casualties. The outrageous number of deaths was racked up only when the battle was essentially over. In other words, as usually happened when one side panicked and ran, the casualties occurred not during the battle but during the chase.

This is a useful distinction, because unless such one-sided contests are separated into two parts—the initial clash and then the chase—they can create the misleading impression that fighting men can be "mown down" (to use a maddeningly overworked phrase) by superior fighters, when in fact soldiers are only mown down when they have dropped all of their defenses. As soon as one army panics and runs, what follows does not properly qualify as battle. As commonly understood, a battle involves fighting, feinting, parrying, thrusting, or at least defending oneself. When an army turns its collective back, however, like the Persians at Marathon or the Romans facing Hannibal at Cannae, the battle proper is over. What follows is merely a slaughter.

Alexander's army at Gaugemela may have been more hardened and professional than most, but it did nothing to disprove the contention that when two armies stand and fight, the death count rises slowly. This explains, for example, why in 480 BC it took six days for a million Persians to defeat 300 Spartans at Thermopylae. (The numbers given here, of course, are wildly exaggerated. They will be placed in proper perspective in Chapter 7.) In hand-to-hand fighting, killing was never accomplished very quickly. Apparently, the reluctance men feel about killing is strongest when they face their opponent, and almost nonexistent when the opponent turns his back. Thus whenever casualties on one side far outweigh those on the other, it is a sure sign of a panic that led to a slaughter of fleeing troops who had thrown down their weapons and discarded all caution.

He Who Leaves a Fight Loses It

In light of the loss of lives it causes, it is not surprising that running away has always not only elicited universal condemnation, but also prompted Draconian measures to insure that it could not or would not happen. Almost all armies, from the Greek phalanxes and Roman legions to modern mechanized forces, adopted strict measures to keep the soldiers in the ranks from throwing down their arms and either surrendering or fleeing. One such method, not usually acknowledged in official histories of wars, called for commanders to threaten to use their weapons on their own troops, and to follow through with the threat if necessary. The sole purpose of many a mounted officer's hand weapon—sword, pontoon, pistol, or pike—was to keep the rear of close-order formations from breaking away. The Roman legionnaire stayed in the ranks, it is said, because he feared his centurion more than any enemy. In imperial armies of the eighteenth and nineteenth centuries, mounted officers used the flat faces of their sword blades to beat men leaving the line. Sometimes those heading to the rear were shot. In his book *Combat Motivation*, Anthony Kellett notes that, "at the turn of the century the image of an officer single-handedly stemming a rout was a well-known literary, historical, and even graphic device." He may have been thinking of Thackeray's Barry Lyndon, who marveled at the fact that in the Prussian army, "there was a corporal to every three men, marching behind them, and pitilessly using the cane; so much so that it used to be said that in action there was a front rank of privates and a second rank of sergeants and corporals to drive them on."

When the situation called for it, some officers could be unsparingly brutal. Kellett relates one incident during the First

World War in which a group of 40 British soldiers facing a German breakthrough threw down their rifles and stood up in their trench in order to surrender. But before they could, the commander of a nearby British machine-gun battalion opened fire on them, claiming afterward, "Such an action as this will in a short time spread like dry rot through an army, and it is one of those dire military necessities which calls for immediate and prompt action. . . . Of a party of forty men who held up their hands, thirty-eight were shot down, with the result that this never occurred again."

Sometimes, of course, a retreat is unavoidable, which raises the question of how, given the contagiousness of terror, it can be carried off without giving way to a panic. It helps not to use the word *retreat* at all. It is so delicate a maneuver, and so tainted with a whiff of disgrace, that it is often thinly disguised as an "advance to the rear." Once pulled off successfully, however, the curtain can be drawn back to reveal the retreat as a masterstroke—proof of military genius.

It is only natural, then, given their rarity, that a few fine retreats should have become legendary to the point of inspiring professional respect even among the enemy. During World War I, for example, Lawrence of Arabia could not conceal his admiration for German units that held together during a rout of their Turkish allies in 1918:

> I grew proud of the enemy who had killed my brothers. They were two thousand miles from home, without hope and without guides, in conditions bad enough to break the bravest nerves. Yet their sections held together, sheering through the wrack of Turk and Arab like armored ships, high-faced and silent. When attacked they halted, took position, fired to order. There was no haste, no crying, no hesitation. They were glorious.

Two thousand miles from home, stranded in Arabia, yet perfectly composed, the Germans would have reminded Lawrence of an army of Greek mercenaries who had pulled off an even more glorious retreat under similar circumstances some 23 centuries earlier. Their exploit, which is to the art of retreat what Leonidas and his Three Hundred are to the last stand, inspired one of the greatest war epics of all time. Lawrence, like generations of commanders before him, knew it well.

Xenophon and the Ten Thousand

In the year 401 BC, a group of Greek mercenaries marched from their homeland to Babylon with Cyrus the Younger, the son of the Persian king Darius II. Cyrus had come to Greece in order to assemble an army with which to overthrow his elder brother, Artaxerxes II, and to seize the throne of Persia. Partly out of respect for this charismatic leader, but mostly for the promise of substantial reward, 10,000 Greeks accompanied Cyrus through Asia Minor and took part in the Battle of Cunaxa (on the Euphrates River near modern-day Baghdad), where they performed spectacularly. Assigned the right flank of the vast attacking force, the Greek phalanx, shouting their fearsome war cry, "Eleleleu," drove Artaxerxes' left wing back several miles, losing only one man of their own while wiping out the enemy. In other words, it was a rout rather than a battle. In the center, Cyrus also fought brilliantly, and drove his way deep into the Persian center to within shouting distance of his brother. But his part of the battle would not end well. The Persians fought back fiercely. As the object of his quest loomed within his grasp, Cyrus threw away all caution, hurled himself into the midst of his brother's imperial guard, and was slain.

Meanwhile, back on the right flank, the Greeks' success had taken them so far into enemy territory that they could not imagine how badly things had gone with Cyrus. It took them two days to realize that he had been killed and the rest of the mercenary army defeated. Yet they mounted a second attack by themselves, and with their phalanx tactics routed the Persians again, after which they faced some difficult decisions. Should they push on and capture Babylon, or should they try to make peace with Artaxerxes? Going home was the least attractive of their options. Home lay 2000 miles away through territories inhabited by many hostile tribes. In the end, the decision was made for them. Their generals, acting under truce as a negotiating team, were tricked and slaughtered by the Persians. Without a leader, the Greeks now had only one option—to retreat in the face of a formidable army through a faraway land, and to try to reach the haven of the Black Sea. Thus the stage was set for one of the great epics of military history.

The best account of the retreat of the Ten Thousand comes from the pen of the man who led it, the Athenian soldier Xenophon, who in his later years turned to reminiscing about war, and thus became one of the greatest historians of ancient Greece. His description of the celebrated retreat, which he entitled the *Anabasis*, turned out to be his magnum opus.

As a writer Xenophon consciously follows the narrative style that his esteemed predecessor Thucydides employed in his chronicle of the Peloponnesian War. Thucydides, another general turned writer, understood that rhetoric drives history (and not the other way around). By reconstructing over 140 speeches, he showed how the Greeks governed by consensus, how they decided matters of state only after a lengthy process of discussion and reasoning. Both writers make it clear that in the Greek world, the art of rhetoric was inextricably linked to the art of war: wars could not occur unless the people could be persuaded to support them; battles could not be won unless one general could convince his fellow generals to adopt his chosen proposed strategy.

Xenophon's Ten Thousand may have been mercenaries, but they were also Greeks, and they were accustomed to being swayed by brilliant speeches. Xenophon reconstructed many such speeches, in which he shows that a leader, faced with the daunting task of organizing a long retreat, must draw upon every kind of motivational device in order to quell the internal squabbling among factions within the army. Not surprisingly, a mercenary force fighting neither for homeland, for glory, or for a higher cause harbored a variety of conflicting agendas. How could such men be inspired? What could Xenophon do to convince them that their only hope of survival lay in staying together? He gives us some idea in the speech he delivers just after having been elected their leader, as he prepares the Ten Thousand for the daunting task that lies ahead:

> And now we must go back and put into execution what has been resolved upon. And whoever among you desires to see his friends again, let him remember to show himself a brave man; for in no other way can he accomplish this desire. Again, whoever is desirous of saving his life, let him strive for victory; for it is the victors that slay and the defeated that are slain. Or if anyone longs for wealth, let him also strive to conquer; for conquerors not only keep their own possessions, but gain the possessions of the conquered.

As their journey wears on, it becomes clear that a controlled retreat must take on the aspect of an invasion in reverse. With no way to establish a supply line to the rear, Xenophon's band had to seek out provisions ahead. Often the local tribes refuse to cooperate, and the Greeks had no option but to go on the attack. In one memorable prebattle speech, Xenophon displays uncharacteristic bluntness when he tells his men that the Colchians are the only thing standing between them and the Black Sea. "If we possibly can," he says, "we must simply eat these fellows raw."

Xenophon wrote the *Anabasis* (also called *The March Up Country*) some 30 years after the event, so we can assume that he took liberties in the retelling. If we can't rely entirely on the accuracy of the speeches or on Xenophon's assessment of his own role, we can at least appreciate the delicacy of the situation. When a formidable army is forced to retreat, its tactics must change. Xenophon's tactical innovation was to arrange his men in a rectangular formation with the baggage and camp followers in the center, an advance guard at the front, two columns forming the sides, and a rear guard consisting of the best fighters led by Xenophon himself. He also adapted to the fighting styles of hostile mountain tribes by imitating them. He discarded the heavy armor of the hoplites in favor of the light arms of archers and spearmen.

The stratagem worked, if only by the sheer willpower of the leader. As he prepared his men for their final battle, Xenophon looked back on what they had accomplished and reminded them that their success depended upon acting the role of the pursuer instead of the pursued. This has turned out to be the key to all successful retreats. He told them that if they could push through to the end, they would earn everlasting fame for what they had done, and he was right. He saw to it personally.

> Soldiers, remember how many battles you have won, with the help of the gods, by coming to close quarters, remember what a fate they suffer who flee from the enemy, and bethink you of this, that we are at the doors of Greece. Follow Heracles the leader and summon one another on, calling each by name. It will surely be sweet, through some manly and noble thing which one may say or do today, to keep himself in remembrance among those whom he wishes to remember him.

Xenophon's *Anabasis* is not merely an adventure story. What sets it on the top shelf of war literature is its psychological realism. Like Thucydides, Xenophon gives short shrift to narrative elements such as scenery, supporting characters, subplots, and other novelistic details. He is more intent on showing what makes men fight or not fight, stand or run. If his descriptions are sometimes unconvincing, it is not because he is trying to elevate the words and deeds of a few main actors to Homeric proportions. What matters to the Greeks is motivation. Although not fully developed, Xenophon's characters at least have recognizably human motives and frailties, and in their plight are caught up in something not entirely in their control. Few cultures since the Greeks have been so deliberate about war; few deliberated about it as much. But their continual striving to understand the why (and not merely the who, what, and when) of warfare explains why the writings of the Greek historians continue to be worth reading.

War and Peace: Bagration at Schön Grabern

The closest modern counterpart to the Greek historians is Leo Tolstoy, whose *War and Peace*, like Xenophon's *Anabasis*, is also a classic tale of retreat, both orderly and disorderly. Although written off by many as the epitome of the overly long Russian novel—an undertaking too large to even consider trying to read—it is actually a very accessible and refreshingly honest book. Its battles are grippingly rendered from an insider's point of view; its characters are psychologically compelling and memorable as individuals. Much like real life, the book has few unambiguous heroes. There are instances of dash and bravado, but they are overshadowed by a quieter sort of courage that admits of human weakness.

The central event in *War and Peace* is Napoleon's march to Moscow in 1812 (which forces a retreat by the Russian army) and his subsequent retreat after the advance stalls. By way of setting the stage for this, Tolstoy begins with the events of seven years earlier, when it was the Russians who marched beyond their borders, only to be sent into a headlong retreat by the lightning maneuvers of Napoleon's generals. This is the action that culminated in the Battle of Austerlitz in 1805, a glorious victory for Napoleon and a disaster for the Russians, but not an unqualified one. For Tolstoy, its one bright, shining moment is a delaying action led by a Russian general noted for his calm disposition. Both the man and the moment might have been forgotten if Tolstoy hadn't plucked them out of obscurity.

The action took place at the village of Schön Grabern (present-day Hollabrunn), just south of Austerlitz, where 4000 men led by Prince Bagration, one of Tolstoy's few unambiguous heroes, held off the entire French army, thus allowing the disordered and dismayed Russian army, under the command of General Kutuzov, to escape. The situation at Schön Grabern was similar to the one Xenophon faced after Cunaxa, and like his venerable predecessor, Bagration handled it brilliantly. Here is how Tolstoy sets the scene:

> Kutuzov sent the adjutants back to hasten to the utmost the movements of the baggage trains of the entire army along the Krems-Znaim road. Bagration's exhausted and hungry detachment which alone covered this movement of the transport and of the whole army, had to remain stationary in face of an enemy eight times as strong as itself. . . . Bonaparte himself, not trusting to his generals, moved with all the Guards to the field of battle, afraid of letting a ready victim escape, and Bagration's four thousand men merrily lighted camp fires, dried and warmed themselves, cooked their porridge for the first time for three days, and not one of them knew or imagined what was in store for him.

Tolstoy had gained firsthand experience of battle by serving as an artillery officer at Sevastopol during the Crimean War, and he held few illusions about war. He had seen bravery in action, but he had also seen stupidity, cowardice, and senseless mayhem. His characterizations of Bagration and Kutuzov lead one to believe that for Tolstoy, a good Russian leader led by inaction—a calm inaction that concedes the impossibility of controlling anything during the heat of battle. It is a view of war so at odds with the typical portrayal of great commanders that it is immediately convincing. We first learn of this counterintuitive style through the observations of Andrew Bolkonsky, Bagration's adjutant.

> Andrew listened attentively to Bagration's colloquies with his commanding officers and the orders he gave them, and to his surprise found that no orders were really given, but that Prince Bagration tried to make it appear that everything done by necessity, by accident, or by the will of subordinate commanders, was done, if not by his direct command, at least in accord with his intentions. Prince Andrew noticed however that though what happened was due to chance and was independent of the commander's will, owing to the tact Bagration showed, his presence was very valuable. Officers who approached him with disturbed countenances became calm; soldiers and officers greeted him gaily, grew more cheerful in his presence, and were evidently anxious to display their courage before him.

The inspired resistance of Bagration's men, and in particular of a small artillery battery, convinces the French that they are fighting the entire Russian army, and not a small rear guard. Unwittingly, perhaps, Tolstoy confirms what we now know about the effects of sustained fire—that fire is best maintained by small clusters of men, that such clusters are effective out of all proportion to their numbers, and that the majority of loosely formed soldiers fire ineffectively, if they fire at all. Bagration seems to know and expect this. He also knows what to do about it. Riding up to his right flank, he comes upon what appears to be total confusion, made even more confused by dense smoke. Some of the men are retreating, some are firing, but it is impossible to tell at whom. The regimental commander explains to the unflappable Bagration that his troops have repelled a cavalry charge, that many have been killed, and that they are now threatened by an approaching line of French infantry. What he is really saying is that he has no control over the situation. Bagration, in his magnanimous way, reacts to the news merely by inclining his head "to signify that this was just as he wished and anticipated," and decides to do the one thing that a good leader can do: rally the men himself.

Like Farragut at New Orleans, Prince Bagration leads with complete disregard for his own safety. He is aware of the danger, but "the pleasant sound of buzzing and whistling bullets" is music to his ears. His subordinates beg him to get out of harm's way, but he doesn't bother to answer them. Instead he orders the infantry into formation along with two cavalry units, and he leads them on with the words, "Keep up your courage, boys!"

> Bagration rode round the ranks that had marched past him and dismounted. He gave the reins to a Cossack, took off and handed over his felt coat, stretched his legs, and set his cap straight. The head of the French column, with its officers leading, appeared from below the hill.
>
> "Forward, with God!" said Bagration in a resolute sonorous voice, turning for a moment to the front line, and, slightly swinging his arms, he went forward uneasily over the rough field with the awkward gait of a cavalryman. . . . Prince Bagration gave no further orders and silently continued to walk on in front of the ranks. Suddenly one shot after another rang out from among the French, smoke appeared all along their uneven ranks, and musket shots sounded. Several of our men fell . . . But at the moment the first report was heard, Bagration looked around and shouted "Hurrah!"
>
> "Hurrah—ah!—ah!" rang a long-drawn shout from our ranks, and passing Bagration and racing one another, they rushed in an irregular but joyous and eager crowd down the hill at their disordered foe.*

---

*This is the action described by the French historian Louis-Adolphe Thiers and mentioned earlier in Chapter 2 as "what seldom happens in war, two bodies of infantry . . . marching resolutely against each other without either of them giving way before meeting."

Meanwhile, the Russian regiment on the far left wing had degenerated into a panicked mob, a phenomenon Tolstoy seems to understand all too well. He notes: "One soldier, in his panic, had shouted the senseless words so terrible in war: 'Cut off!' and these words, with the accompanying panic, had spread through the whole troop." The regimental commander on that wing, leading an overextended cavalry charge into the French ranks, sensed his men's predicament and rode back to stem the flow of retreat. But he had none of Bagration's calm, and the situation slipped away from him.

> That moment of moral vacillation had arrived which decides the fate of a battle: would these scattered throngs of soldiers heed their commander's voice, or would they merely look at him and pursue their way? Notwithstanding the despairing shouts of their general, which had hitherto been so terrible to them, notwithstanding his infuriated, purple face, so unlike its ordinary appearance, and notwithstanding his brandished sword, the soldiers still persisted in the flight, shouted, fired their guns into the air, and paid no heed to the command. The moral balance, which decides the destinies of battles, had evidently kicked the beam on the side of panic.

It is easy to see what causes a panic after the fact. Not so obvious is how to head one off. The writer John Baynes (in *Morale: A Study of Men and Courage*) recounts an episode of the First World War in which a soldier started a panic by shouting: "Get out! Get out! We're all going to be killed!" just as a German attack began. A sergeant cut off the panic and the instigator by splitting his skull open with a shovel. S.L.A. Marshall, noting similar episodes in the Second World War, believed that a panic often resulted from an overreaction to an order to withdraw or to an unexpected threat. Sometimes the threat was nothing more than an illusion.

Not surprisingly, good communication is the key to heading off such overreactions. "The role of the commander," wrote Charles Ardant du Picq, as though he had Bagration in mind, "is to maintain morale, to direct those movements which men instinctually execute when engaged and under pressure of danger." But mere words cannot tip the moral balance when there is no self-control. This is apparent in the contrast between Bagration and the regimental commander. As Field Marshall Montgomery has noted, "A commander, besides commanding his armies, has got to learn how to command *himself*—which is not always too easy." By exploring such insights Tolstoy presents war with a realism we expect from historians but usually fail to get.

Bagration's happy few succeeded at their mission, although with heavy losses. They delayed Napoleon's army, but only for a while. Kutuzov reluctantly agreed to end his retreat and face the French at Austerlitz, but it proved to be a catastrophe for Russia and its allies. Tolstoy takes great pains to explain why, but one question lingers long after the smoke has cleared: how could so few do so well against so many, as Bagration had shown at Schön Grabern, and then suffer a humiliating defeat shortly thereafter, when their numbers had grown to match that of the enemy? Andrew Bolkonsky, Bagration's adjutant and another of Tolstoy's heroes, struggled to understand it, but could only conclude that "sometimes— when there is not a coward at the front to shout, 'We are cut off' and start running, but a brave and jolly lad who shouts 'Hurrah!'—a detachment of five thousand is worth thirty thousand, as at Schön Grabern, while at times fifty thousand run from eight thousand as at Austerlitz." It is an interesting point, and one deserving a chapter of its own.

Now, my gallant fellows, what though we be a small body when compared to the army of our enemies; do not let us be cast down on that account, for victory does not always follow numbers, but where the Almighty God wishes to bestow it.

Prince Edward (The Black Prince)
Battle of Poitiers
17 September 1356

If our number is small, our hearts are great.

Sir Henry Morgan
Siege of Porto Bello
26 June 1668

Though we number only one hundred knights we have got to defeat this large army. Before they reach the plain we shall attack with our lances. For each man you strike, three saddles will go empty.

El Cid

Never fight against heavy odds, if by any possible maneuvering you can hurl your own force on only a part, and that the weakest part, of your enemy and crush it. Such tactics will win every time, and a small army may thus destroy a large one in detail, and repeated victory will make it invincible.

Stonewall Jackson
Rules of War

We are so outnumbered there's only one thing to do. We must attack.

Sir Andrew Browne Cunningham
Torpedo assault on the Italian fleet at Taranto
11 November 1940

"Already distressed." The not-so-few, not-so-happy French knights on the morning of the Battle of Agincourt, October 25, 1415. From a drawing by Alphonse de Neuville.

CHAPTER SEVEN

We Few, We Happy Few

THE UNRELIABILITY OF NUMBERS
IN HISTORY

The Advantage of Being Outnumbered

One of the high points of any production of Shakespeare's *Henry* V is the Saint Crispin's day speech at the Battle of Agincourt, in which the English king rhapsodizes over the glorious plight of his vastly outnumbered army with the words, "We few, we happy few, we band of brothers." What prompts this outpouring of fraternal emotion is the Earl of Westmoreland's complaint that if only they had "ten thousand of those men in England that do no work today," they would at least have a fighting chance. But Henry will have none of that, and delivers his justly famous rejoinder:

> If we are marked to die, we are enow
>
> To do our country loss; and if to live,
>
> The fewer men, the greater share of honor.
>
> God's will! I pray thee wish not one man more.

This is usually assumed to be a show of stoic bravado that harks back to the prebattle speeches recorded by ancient historians (notably Thucydides and Xenophon), speeches in which an outnumbered force cement their solidarity by reveling in their numerical disadvantage. "The fewer men, the greater the honor" was by Shakespeare's time a well-known proverb, trotted out in many instances of the glorious, fighting few. In Froissart's account of the Battle of Poitiers in 1356, for example, the Prince of Wales harangues his men prior to the battle in a speech that closely parallels Henry's. Shakespeare was undoubtedly familiar with it.

> Now, my gallant fellows, what though we be a small body when compared to the army of our enemies; do not let us be cast down on that account, for victory does not always follow numbers, but where the Almighty God wishes to bestow it. If, through good fortune, the day shall be ours, we shall gain the greatest honor and glory in this world: if the contrary should happen, and we be slain, I have a father and beloved brethren alive, and you all have some relations, or good friends, who will be sure to revenge our deaths. I therefore entreat of you to exert yourselves, and combat manfully; for, if it please God and St. George, you shall see me this day act like a true knight.

Of course the race does not always go to the swift nor the battle to the stronger in number. Despite being outmanned, both King Henry and Prince Edward managed to prevail quite handily due to the incompetence of their opponents. In each instance, the French squandered their numerical advantage by charging before they were ready, by bunching up, and by underestimating the range and accuracy of the English longbow. The numbers not only fail to tell the whole story, but they actually obscure it. Ten thousand more men might actually have hindered the English, whereas fewer men (and less overconfidence) might have saved the French. It seems that in war, as these and many other examples show, strength is not always proportional to size.

Effectives and Effectiveness

Numbers in warfare are almost always misleading. When they are not wildly inaccurate, which is often the case, they can hide crucial distinctions. The ancient Persians, for example, never fielded an army a million strong, or anything close to it. Yet in rapturous accounts of Alexander the Great's campaigns, we are told exactly that, even though it flies in the face of everything known about Persian society, if not the logistical reality of organizing anything on a large scale. To say that 40,000 Macedonians defeated a million Persians at Gaugemela (in 331 BC) with practically no losses is to reduce history to fantasy. Rather than telling us what really happened, it prevents us from looking further. The numbers supposedly prove that superior generalship and more disciplined troops made the difference, which was in fact the case. But against a million fighting men?

Nothing epitomizes more succinctly the problem of numbers in history than the use of the word *effective* in descriptions of battles. Although merely an adjective in Shakespeare's time, the word would soon evolve into the noun that we still use today to describe any soldier who is available and ready for combat. Few historians, if any, use the term with any sense of irony; but perhaps they should start, because the very presumption of "readiness" makes every use of the word a distortion of history. It is one thing to report how large an army was or how many men marched off to battle, but to leave out the fact that tens of thousands of soldiers on both sides were lost in the shuffle (literally and figuratively) hardly makes for "effective" history writing.

In 1812, Napoleon crossed into Russia with over 600,000 men, but by the time he fought the Battle of Borodino, he was down to about 100,000 "effectives." Of these, tens of thousands did not take part in the battle. Among them were Napoleon's Old Guard, whom he kept in reserve even though they might have made a difference. Similarly, he began his Austrian campaign of 1805 with over 200,000 men, but had only 73,000 to draw upon at the Battle of Austerlitz. Of these, many saw no action at all. At Waterloo, we are told, the Duke of Wellington had 68,000 British troops available at the outset. This figure is accurate enough. What we are rarely told is that at least 15,000 of these men did not take part in the fighting for various reasons. Nor are we told that this is typical. Out of all the warriors available to serve in a war or fight in a battle, a significant percentage never do any fighting or have any effect on the outcome. In other words, numbers alone do not tell the story.

At Arques in 1589, Henry IV, the French Huguenot king, led 9,000 men against 20,000 Catholics under the Duke de Mayenne, and won. Without more details, we are forced to conclude that each of Henry's soldiers took on two of the enemy, or fought twice as hard. The reality is less far-fetched. Like his namesake at Agincourt, the French Henry negated the numerical superiority of his opponent by choosing the terrain and limiting the battle to a narrow front, in which only a few thousand men could come into contact. Using superior tactics, his troops dominated this front, and wore down and eventually killed more of the enemy than their own number, thus forcing a surrender. This does not mean that each Huguenot killed two or more Catholics, or that at Agincourt each Englishman brought down five Frenchmen. Nor, more importantly, does it mean that every man present actually fought. What it does indicate is something the two Henrys knew very well: that not all "effectives" are equally effective. Some men run, some hide, some avoid killing, some are held in reserve, and some never make it to the front. Some can even be a hindrance if they cannot be brought to bear on the enemy. All of this helps to explain one of the more puzzling battle orders in all of history, and one of the oldest—the dismissal of part of the army before an impending battle.

Gideon's Raid

Of the many battles described in the Bible, none is quite as memorable as Gideon's nighttime raid on the Midian camp as recounted in the Book of Judges. As with many stories in the Bible, what we are told is interesting, but what we are not told is intriguing. Briefly stated, back in the eleventh century BC, a tribe of desert raiders called the Midians descended each year upon Israelite settlements in northern Palestine and subjugated the people to a reign of terror. Anticipating this seasonal visitation, the Jewish warrior Gideon was able to unite the dispersed Israelites and raise a large army numbering 32,000. But it was hardly a reliable force. Most of them were not fighters, and numerous as they were, they were no match for the Midians, at least until the Lord of the Israelites appeared to Gideon with some unusual instructions. First he told Gideon to dismiss all those who wished to return home. It sounded like madness, but Gideon obeyed and sent home 22,000 "effectives." But the Lord was not satisfied and proposed another test that would reduce the force even more. Each man was to be observed drinking from a stream near the Midian encampment. Those who turned their backs and lapped up the water like dogs would be dismissed, while those who brought the water up to their mouths would be retained. All but 300 of the men failed this test of alertness, and so it was with this select band that Gideon staged his famous nighttime raid.

The plan was simple: Gideon divided his band into three companies each a hundred strong, and instructed each man to carry a trumpet and an earthen jar containing a torch. When they heard him give the signal with his trumpet, they were all to blow their trumpets and yell out their battle cry: "The sword of the Lord, and of Gideon." As we are told in Judges:

> So Gideon and the hundred men that were with him came unto the outside of the camp in the beginning of the middle watch . . . and they blew the trumpets and brake the pitchers, and held the lamps in their left hands and the trumpets in their right hands to blow withal, and they cried, The sword of the Lord, and of Gideon . . .

113

In the confusion the Midians were easy prey. They even attacked each other, and the Israelites easily drove them across the river and destroyed them.

By way of explanation, the Bible states that the God of the Israelites wanted nothing to detract from his own role in the great battle. If an army of 32,000 or even 10,000 had defeated the Midians, the glory would have belonged to the men. But if 300 defeated the host of invaders, it could only redound to the greater glory of God. There is, however, a more practical explanation.

Gideon knew that he could not rely on most of the men in his army. As great generals have suspected since the very origins of organized warfare, and as S.L.A. Marshall and Charles Ardant du Picq would later make painfully clear, natural fighters comprise less than a quarter of any army, and sometimes not even that. Consequently, small armies can and do defeat large ones. The reasons for this are fairly obvious. One is that size is inversely related to mobility and stealth. The larger the army, the more ponderous; it can move neither very quickly nor with much secrecy. On the other hand, the smaller the force, the more efficiently it can carry out maneuvers, and with a lower risk of discovery. Gideon's band, for example, sneaked into the Midian camp and executed a surprise maneuver that would have failed disastrously if it had been given away in advance or if the men had not synchronized the surprise.

Another reason small armies often prevailed is selectivity. Gideon reduced the size of his army in order to weed out unreliable fighters. Napoleon occasionally did the same, sending home thousands of unwilling conscripts, most of whom he knew would desert anyway. As du Picq noted:

> It is not wise to lead eighty thousand men upon the battlefield, of whom but fifty thousand will fight. It would be better to have fifty thousand, all of whom would fight. These fifty thousand would have their hearts in their work more than the others, who should have con-

fidence in their comrades but cannot when one third of them shrink from their work.

In the book of Deuteronomy, we are told of certain Israelite generals who did much the same thing. They freely dismissed newly wed soldiers, family men, and farmers—in short, those who had something to lose. Although often misinterpreted as a liberal policy of conscription, it was nothing but a practical measure that even Shakespeare's Henry V appreciated: those who have no zest for the fight will be a burden to the rest. Better to let them go. As the king says to the Earl of Westmoreland on the morning of Agincourt, "He which hath no stomach to this fight, let him depart: his passport shall be made, and crowns for convoy put into his purse."

Gideon's 300, like the small, efficient, and highly mobile armies of Judas Maccabias that attained similar successes centuries later (and are chronicled in the First Book of Maccabees), proved that strength is not simply a matter of size. Selectivity, training, organization, and strong leadership are more important. On the other hand, large armies facing smaller ones can and do become convinced of their superiority, and this conceit often provides the recipe for upset victories.

The Battle Royal

If dismissing unreliable fighters seems a sensible idea, why not carry it to its logical conclusion and have both sides be represented by their most willing men? The idea is intriguing: if each of the warring factions will agree to select an equal number of their best men, the resulting contest will prove beyond a doubt which side is the most deserving. The arrangement is called a battle royal, and while such contests have been described, it is not clear that one ever took place.

What little evidence we have of such contests is not entirely reliable. For example, one of the most celebrated battle royals occurs at the climax of Sir Walter Scott's *Fair Maid of Perth*, a tale allegedly woven from a skein of real events. In the novel, 30 members of the Clan Chattan square off against 30 of the Clan Quhele in the Combat at the Inch of Perth, as it is called. In some details it closely parallels an equally well-known battle royal, the so-called Battle of the Thirty, a fourteenth-century encounter between 30 Breton and 30 English knights mentioned by the French chronicler Froissart. In each case a good deal of grunting and hacking, punctuated by time-outs, resulted in . . . nothing particularly decisive when all was said and done. Both battles ended more or less in a standoff, which seems to be the problem with fights of this type. When the dust settles, it is often difficult to say who won.

This difficulty is vividly illustrated by what has to be the greatest battle royal of all time, a showdown between the Argives and the Spartans as described by Herodotus in his *Histories.*

> The Argives collected troops to resist the seizure of Thyrea, but before any battle was fought, the two parties came to terms, and it was agreed that 300 Spartans and 300 Argives should meet and fight for the place, which should belong to the nation with whom the victory rested. It was stipulated also that other troops on each side should return home to their respective countries, and not remain to witness the combat, as there was danger, if the armies stayed, that either the one or the other, on seeing their countrymen undergoing defeat, might hasten to their assistance. These terms being agreed on, the two armies marched off, leaving 300 picked men on each side to fight for the territory. The battle began, and so equal were the combatants, that at the close of the day, when night put a stop to the fight, of the whole 600 only three men remained alive, two Argives . . . and a single Spartan.

As in most modern-day tag-team matches, the result was inconclusive. The two Argives, assuming the victory belonged to them, hurried back to Argos with the news. Meanwhile, the lone surviving Spartan stripped the armor off the fallen Argives and brought it to the Spartan camp. When the two armies reconvened, they argued over which side deserved the victory—the side with more survivors, or the side that held the field at the end. Naturally, the discussion degenerated into an argument, words gave way to blows, and both armies squared off once again. When the dust cleared, the Spartans, having inflicted a few more casualties than they suffered, managed to limp off with the prize.

The Cult of the Three Hundred

As much as we might want to believe the story of the Spartans and the Argives, there are good reasons not to. Foremost among them is Herodotus' habit of placing the requirements of good storytelling above the demands of authenticity. Take, for example, his strange affinity for the number 300. When he needed a large number, it sometimes seems, he reached for a million, and when he needed a small one he almost always used 300.

There is no evidence that Herodotus knew the story of Gideon's band, so it may simply be a coincidence that in his *Histories* he uses the number 300 on several occasions to describe a cohort of the "best and the bravest." Just prior to the Battle of Plataea in 479 BC, in which the Greeks expelled the remnants of the Persian invasion force that survived the Battle of Salamis, the Megarian infantry came under a Persian cavalry attack and called for help. None were willing to go until "the Athenians offered themselves; and a body of picked men, 300 in number, commanded by Olympiodorus . . . undertook the service." Later, during the battle itself, the Spartan Aeimnestus killed the Persian general Mardonius, thus avenging the slaughter of Leonidas and the celebrated 300 at Thermopylae. With an unmistakable flair for symmetry, Herodotus notes that Aeimnestus would later lead 300 men against a larger force of Messenians, and all would perish. Meanwhile, still at Plataea, we are told of "300 of the best and bravest" among the Thebans who fought on the Persian side and were slain by the Athenians. (In the same battle Aristodemus, the only survivor among Leonidas' 300, the man who because of temporary blindness seized a chance to return home, sought to atone for his shame by stepping out of the ranks and fighting like a madman. Yet, as Herodotus notes, "Aristodemus alone had no honors, because he courted death." That is, he shamed himself again by leaving the battle formation.)

Herodotus did not grab the number 300 out of thin air. It was, he explains, the size of a Spartan royal bodyguard. Thus it was natural for Leonidas to take that number with him to Thermopylae, and wise of him to take no more. Sparta was not a large city and could spare only a small cohort for what Leonidas understood might well be a suicide mission. We can accept the number 300 in this instance because the names of these men were later inscribed on a monument that Herodotus inspected personally. His use of the number elsewhere may simply have been an act of homage. Besides, small forces were routinely and quite reasonably rounded off in accounts of battle. The 673 members of the Light Brigade, for example, bowed to the necessity of poetic meter to become Tennyson's "noble six hundred."

It is in the realm of large numbers, however, that Herodotus completely lost touch with physical reality, and in so doing set an unfortunate precedent. Generations of historians not only took him at his word, but compounded his mistakes with exaggerations of their own. Surprisingly, it was not until a century ago that anyone thought to seriously question numbers that are too far off to be excused by poetic license.

Hans Delbrück's Crusade for Truth in Numbers

Since the time of Herodotus, it had been accepted as an article of faith that the Greeks who repelled the Persian invasion at Marathon were vastly outnumbered. What makes this contention so sacrosanct is the symbolic weight placed on this one battle. It is the first of Sir Edward Creasy's "Fifteen Decisive Battles of the World," chosen because it decided the course of Western civilization, or so it seems. The "what if" faction weighs in heavily on the Battle of Marathon, asserting that if the Greeks had lost, Athens would never have produced its golden age of art and philosophy, and the entire Western tradition—the Socratic method, Aristotelian empiricism, the classical orders of architecture—might have been lost. Creasy, who confidently numbered the Greek army at 10,000 and the Persian invasion force at ten times that number, declared that the Greek victory "secured for mankind the intellectual treasures of Athens, the growth of free institutions, the liberal enlightenment of the Western world, and the gradual ascendancy for many ages of the great principles of European civilization." Thus not only was victory essential, but in retrospect it had to be a decisive victory against seemingly overwhelming odds. Moreover, it had to look preordained. After Herodotus, Western historians insisted upon sustaining this claim, at least until Hans Delbrück came along.

The German historian Hans Delbrück is one of those forgotten thinkers who spent a lifetime trying to convince the defenders of conventional history to accept logical propositions that now cause us no anxiety, but that once were considered heretical. No one today takes great offense at being told that Alexander the Great was not outnumbered at the Granicus River, or that Frederick the Great favored the strategy of war by attrition in his later battles. But this was not the case a century ago. Some truths were assumed to be self-evident and sacrosanct. In his 40 years as a professor at the University of Berlin, Delbrück waded against the current of received ideas as he

119

tried to establish a scientific basis for the study of military history. The effort won him few friends and no immediate followers, but today he is regarded as a pioneer—the first to consider what is physically possible and not possible in battle.

Delbrück's method is best illustrated by one of his most famous arguments, that Herodotus grossly overestimated the size of the Persian land force that invaded Greece ten years after the Battle of Marathon. This was the army that Leonidas hoped to stop at Thermopylae. Herodotus lists the strength of each division, leaving it to the reader to tally it up and arrive at a total of over four million, including attendants. The number is impressive, but impossible. Delbrück points out that a modern German army of 30,000 in march formation covers 14 miles, not including its supply train. By a simple extrapolation, he argues, the head of the Persian column (as described by Herodotus) would just be reaching Thermopylae as its tail was leaving Susa, some 2000 miles away. Scholars have subsequently rounded down the strength of Xerxes' army to about 100,000, although Delbrück pegs it even lower.

Not all of Herodotus' numbers, in Delbrück's opinion, fall quite so wide of the mark, but they are still dangerously misleading. At the Battle of Plataea in 479 BC, the Greek historian gives a figure of 300,000 for the Persian force, to which Delbrück objects, pointing out that the maneuvers Mardonius' army made would not have been possible for a force much larger than 75,000 men, given the terrain. As Delbrück famously observed, "A movement that is made by an organization of 1000 men without complications becomes an accomplishment for 10,000 men, a work of art for 50,000, and an impossibility for 100,000."

To those of us who quickly tire of clinically precise battle synopses that matter-of-factly affix troop strengths as confidently as ship tonnages and that credit upset victories to technical genius alone, Delbrück's analyses come as a breath of fresh air. He points out, for example, that the Gauls of Caesar's day could not have fielded large armies, despite their reputation for doing so. They had the manpower, but not the level of social organization that would have allowed it. Nor could the ancient Persians, given the nature of their society, have assembled million-man armies against the Greeks. All of this makes sense once we allow ourselves to consider the logistics, which few history books encourage us to do.

Classicists and other historians of Delbrück's day erupted over such dispassionate arguments. They accused him of trashing their revered classical authors, going so far as to claim that he ignored the substantial military assistance rendered by the Greek gods! The Athenians could indeed, as Herodotus has it, have sprinted over a mile in full armor over the plain of Marathon, they say, because the goddess Artemis aided them. But once we suppress the proprietary emotions that war can incite, we have to side with Delbrück. The Greek hoplites could not have sustained a running charge of much more than 200 yards. They were not grossly outnumbered. The Spartans did not hold the pass at Thermopylae with a mere 300 men, nor did Persia ever amass an army numbering even close to a million. Why have we been so quick to accept these numbers? Delbrück argues that it is because the public is and has always been unable to rise above certain simplistic stereotypes:

> The victory of the citizen armies over the professional army has been distorted in the Greek legend, which is our only source, into the victory of a small minority over a gigantic majority. This is a national psychological aberration that one finds again and again. The criterion of quality is too fine for the mass, which transforms it into the criterion of quantity.

The Persians were a formidable opponent, which made them loom larger in size than in skill once they had been defeated. In short, Delbrück concludes, "victory of a small force over a vastly superior one is simply the basic manner in which the crowd pictures heroic deeds and strategic genius."

Delbrück was the first modern historian to deal with the question of numbers in history, and remains one of the few. He begins his magnum opus, the four-volume *History of the Art of War*, with the statement: "Whenever the sources permit, a military-historical study does best to start with the army strengths. They are of decisive importance." And yet, like National Park Service officials who have the thankless job of estimating the number of demonstrators who march on Washington, he was well aware how difficult such head-counting could be: "To count an army accurately is not as easy as one might think, even for its commander. If he is satisfied with adding up the reports of his subordinate commanders . . . the question arises whether these reports are reliable."

It seems likely that most commanders counted not heads, but regiments. This explains why army strengths are almost always given in thousands. It helps to remember that the root of the word *military* is *miles*, the Latin for a thousand. It derives from the idea that each soldier was chosen out of a thousand Roman citizens, but it also happens to describe the ideal size of a regiment, a fact that might explain some of the overestimation in army sizes. Few regiments have ever been able to maintain their full strength. The Light Brigade at Balaclava numbered fewer than 700. At Little Round Top in the Civil War, both the 15th Alabama and the 20th Maine regiments numbered about 400 men—a typical regiment size in that war and many others. By relying only on counts of regiments, it is easy to see how a general could arrive at a figure of 30,000 when he in fact had only 20,000.

When they were not miscounting, many generals were purposely misleading us. In their memoirs, Julius Caesar, Frederick the Great, and Napoleon (among many others) routinely tweaked the numbers for self-serving reasons, and most historians have been sucked into taking them at their word. It is only natural to overestimate the size of the enemy one has just defeated and to understate the size of one's own gallant band of brothers, and not simply for political reasons. For one thing, it makes for a livelier story; but there were also tactical motives. If opposing generals came to believe such stories they would exercise more caution, especially when deciding whether they should attempt to follow up on a local victory. Napoleon in particular understood that a reputation founded upon lies is far more useful than one based on the truth.

Hans Delbrück tried to set the record straight. By applying scientific methods of historical reconstruction, including logistical considerations, population estimates, and social structures, he managed to deflate not only Herodotus' overestimates, but those of Caesar, Frederick, and Napoleon, along with the pronouncements of generations of historians who have accepted the generals' most outrageously self-serving lies. Delbrück would pay a price for doing so. By challenging notions that traditional historians viewed as sacred truths, he managed to bring a wave of derision and scorn crashing down upon his head. His professional advancement was thwarted, and he was put down as an amateur and a crank. But thanks to his persistence we can now entertain plausible conjectures that were considered heretical a century ago. Perhaps the most controversial of these is Delbrück's claim that, instead of being woefully outnumbered by the Persians at the Battle of Marathon, the Greeks probably enjoyed a slight edge.

In the case of the Battle of Marathon, as in so many other famous battles, a comparison of the numbers given in standard reference works reveals some serious discrepancies. *The Harper Encyclopedia of Military History*, Harbottle's *Dictionary of Battles*, Eggenberger's *Dictionary of Battles*, and the encyclopedias *Americana* and *Britannica*, for example, accept Herodotus' figures: 11,000 Greek heavy infantry (hoplites), 192 Greek dead, and 6200 Persian dead. Yet the numbers they give for the Persian invading force (a number that Herodotus did not specify) range from a low of 15,000 to Creasy's estimate of 100,000, which he passes on rather uncritically from the third-century Roman historian Justin. At least one respectable source places the number as high as 200,000. Disappointingly, the otherwise reliable and insightful John Keegan, in his *History of Warfare*, gives a figure of 50,000, whereas in his earlier *Face of Battle* he endorses an estimate of 25,000.

Most scholarly disciplines would not tolerate such discrepancies, but in military history they are all too common and all too rarely criticized. Delbrück visited the battlefields, pored over the texts, analyzed the archaeological evidence, and used scientific methods to produce highly probable estimates of army strengths. When no conclusion was possible, he said as much. Here are his conclusions about Marathon:

> On the basis of the previously discussed relationships [namely the size of the battlefield, the total population of the respective societies, the battle tactics employed, and the number of casualties], we estimate the Persian army in 490 BC at about the same strength as the Athenians or perhaps somewhat smaller—that is, about 4,000 to 6,000 warriors, including 500 to 800 mounted men. And in addition, as with the Greeks, there was a large number of unarmored men.

As for the casualties, Delbrück estimates that the number of dead, given the nature of Greek armor and weaponry, should amount to about one-fifth of the number wounded. Thus 200 dead would indicate about 1000 wounded. "Concerning the losses of the Persians," he concedes, "we have no reliable figure."

What is refreshing about Delbrück's analysis is its unprecedented candor. Some things, such as the number of Persian casualties, we not only do not know, but have no way of guessing. He also brings into the equation a key factor that Herodotus and his followers leave out: the presence of fighters who were not counted as full citizens. The typical Greek hoplite was accompanied by at least one assistant who helped him with his armor and carried his weapons. To what extent these attendants participated in the fighting is not clear.

Neither is the role of lightly armed men of lower social standing, some of them slaves, who were never included in troop strength estimates or in body counts. Such men took part as "effectives" in all ancient battles, yet their role in war is as unacknowledged as it was in Greek society. What comes out of this analysis is a picture that is, for once, believable. We no longer have to suspend all of our disbelief in trying to understand one of history's most famous clashes.

In addition to estimating army strengths, Delbrück was keen to discover what percentage of the men present at battles actually took part in the fighting. The classic battle piece focuses so intently on the action that it misses the lack of it, thus reinforcing the patently false notion that everyone is slugging it out. Delbrück provides one example that should at least make us question the physical possibility of this. It concerns the logistical nightmare of deploying large numbers of soldiers so as to bring them into contact with the enemy. A sweeping arrow arcing across a map may nicely summarize a flanking maneuver, but what is the human reality hidden behind that arrow?

At the Battle of the Granicus River in 334 BC, Alexander the Great faced what was reputed to be a larger Persian force, although the consensus now seems to be that the opposing forces were equally matched, each numbering about 40,000. Until recently, this had been touted as yet another brilliant shorthanded victory. But after careful analysis, Delbrück concludes that "the real battle was carried out by no more than some 6000 men." This is no small point: 80,000 men meet on a battlefield but only 6000 of them do any real fighting. That constitutes the whole battle. We should not be tempted to apply this formula to all battles, but it seems safe to say, as Delbrück does, that it is not physically possible for everyone present to engage the enemy, nor should we automatically assume that the same proportion of each opposing army participated in the fighting. We also have to be skeptical about most estimates of casualties. At the Granicus, Delbrück notes, the 20,000 Greek mercenaries in the pay of the Persians, a force reputed to have been slaughtered by the Macedonians, probably did not fight at all. Slaughtering 20,000 men is not a simple matter. It is far more likely that the Greeks surrendered instead.

The point is not that all estimates of army strengths are way off, or that victorious underdogs are never really outnumbered, or even, as at the Granicus, that most soldiers do not fight. Rather, the point is that we should not let numbers cloud our understanding of the human element in warfare. "Leonidas and the Three Hundred" does sound better than "Leonidas, the Three Hundred Spartans, the Thousand Thespians, the many Helots, and the Few Hundred Others Who Stuck It Out." We hear only about the 300, but we should take note that there were others present—perhaps as many as 7000 for the first three days, and at least 1000 for the last three. We are told that they faced an army more than a million strong, but this is physically impossible. The inquiring reader should be relieved not to have to swallow such a figure. It is far more reassuring to learn that the Persian army numbered no more than 100,000. (The story is sketched in more detail in Chapters 8 and 10.)

Above all, it is safe to say that all numbers in history should be approached with caution. Large numbers are notoriously unreliable, if only because most people have such a poor concept of number to begin with. It is also useful, when contemplating a shorthanded victory, to reflect upon an observation made by the seventeenth-century cavalry officer, the Count of Montecuccoli, who wrote: "Battle is fought more with the mind than with the body, and therefore a large number is not always useful." The plight of the few against the many is an inspiring pose, but was often beside the point. As Maurice de Saxe asserted, "It is better to have a small number of well-kept and well-disciplined troops than to have a great number who are neglected in these matters. It is not big armies that win battles; it is good ones."

Tell him to go to hell.

General Zachary Taylor
Reaction to Santa Anna's surrender demand
Battle of Buena Vista (Mexican-American War)
22 February 1847

Nuts!

General Anthony C. McAuliffe
Reply to the German surrender demand at Bastogne
Battle of Ardennes II
22 December 1944

The Guard dies; it never surrenders!

General Pierre Cambronne
Refusal to surrender at the Battle of Waterloo
18 July 1815

Send more Japs.

The Marine garrison
Alleged report to headquarters after repulsing a Japanese attack
Wake Island
11 December 1941

Go howl.

Idanthyrsus, king of the Scythians
To Darius the Great of Persia
Herodotus, *Histories*

I have not yet begun to fight.

John Paul Jones
Battle of Flamborough Head
23 September 1779

John Paul Jones and the crew of the Bonhomme Richard at the Battle of Flamborough Head. An illustration from Harper's Magazine.

CHAPTER EIGHT

I Have Not Yet Begun to Fight!

THE ANNALS OF DEFIANCE FROM THERMOPYLAE TO WATERLOO

Bastogne

In the autumn of 1944 Europe braced for the last major show-down of the Second World War. As the Soviet army broke through Eastern Poland and as Allied forces swept eastward through France into Belgium, the German high command staged a major offensive, their last, in the form of a counterat-tack through the Ardennes forest, with the port of Antwerp as their ultimate objective. Despite a determined effort, they would not reach it. Their defeat in the Battle of the Bulge would hasten their demise in a war that was essentially already lost.

Although it lasted almost two months; involved about three-quarters of a million combatants in armored, airborne, artillery, and infantry units; and consisted of an uncountable number of individual actions, the Ardennes campaign pro-duced one signal incident, centering of all things on one word of one syllable—a word that stands out as the defining symbol not only of the conflict, but of the entire war. It happened in the Belgian village of Bastogne, a strategically important cross-roads tenuously held by the 101st Airborne Division under the command of Anthony C. McAuliffe, a 46-year-old West Point graduate and brigadier general.

A dramatic standoff materialized at Bastogne when the 101st, which had parachuted into Normandy on D-Day, pressed eastward as German armored divisions knifed westward, resulting in a precarious overlap at this key village. McAuliffe's men had raced into the town just ahead of the Germans, but were ill-equipped to face down the Panzer units lurking a few miles away. On December 19, the American position started to look somewhat desperate, and McAuliffe began to circle the wagons.

The scene inside the town itself was chaotic. Men who had been separated from their companies, survivors of shattered units, wounded and dying soldiers, frightened civilians, and a confusion of vehicles and supplies added up to a logistical nightmare. Ironically, the fact that Bastogne was nearly surrounded brought McAuliffe a measure of relief by eliminating the one option he dreaded most—having to pull out. Knowing that George Patton's 4th Armored Division would eventually be coming his way, McAuliffe decided to make a stand rather than risk the heavy losses that are inevitable in a retreat. As he put it, if he pulled out, his division would be "cut to pieces."

Meanwhile General Heinrich von Luettwitz, commanding two Panzer corps outside of Bastogne, faced a different dilemma. The German high command had decided to bypass the town and left it up to Luettwitz to take Bastogne with whatever he had. It wasn't much. Although he was promised some reinforcements, Luettwitz was underequipped for the kind of attack that would guarantee success, and he needed to act fast. So he hatched a bold ploy.

On the morning of December 22, four German soldiers approached an American outpost carrying a white flag and a typewritten message (apparently in English and in German) addressed to "The U.S.A. Commander in the Encircled Town of Bastogne." It read:

> The fortune of war is changing. This time, the U.S. forces in and near Bastogne have been encircled by strong German armored units. . . . There is only one possibility of saving the encircled U.S.A. troops from annihilation. That is the honorable surrender of the encircled town. In order to think it over, a term of two

hours shall be granted, beginning with the presentation of this note. If this proposal is rejected, one German artillery corps and six heavy antiaircraft batteries are ready to annihilate the U.S.A. forces in and near Bastogne. The order for firing will be given immediately after the two hours' term. All serious civilian casualties caused by this artillery fire would not correspond with well-known American humanity.

The note was signed, rather ambiguously, "The German commander."

According to official accounts of the incident, McAuliffe reacted in disgust when handed the note, saying, "Ah, nuts!" He had no way of knowing that Luettwitz was bluffing, that he didn't have the antiaircraft batteries to back up his threat. With all the enthusiasm of a child writing a thank-you note for an unwanted gift, McAuliffe put off replying. "I don't know what the hell to say to them," he muttered, presumably meaning that he knew exactly what to say but was reluctant to put it in writing. His planning officer, Lieutenant Colonel Kinnard, then offered a helpful suggestion.

> "Sir, that first remark of yours would be pretty hard to beat."
> "What did I say?"
> "Nuts."

Moments later, Colonel Joseph Harper arrived at division command to pick up a communiqué typed on 8- by 11-inch bond paper. McAuliffe told him to see that it was delivered. Harper read it, smiled, and said he would do so personally. If it still exists, this document, letter for letter, would fetch a price on a par with the notebooks of DaVinci. Its entire text read:

> To the German Commander:
> Nuts!
> The American Commander

There's more to the story, although this alone was enough to make McAuliffe an instant legend. Rumors of the incident spread quickly through Bastogne, building priceless reserves of morale. Later, the story blazed over the wire services and came to exemplify the American effort. But how accurate is it? Admittedly, we will never know all of the facts, much less the nuances. Luettwitz conceded, much later, that he had indeed issued an ultimatum without authority from his superiors, and McAuliffe (of course) rejected it out of hand. As for the particulars, they are plausible. But if the American general had tried to put it in historical perspective, he might have been struck with a strange sense of déjà vu. Hadn't this happened before? Hadn't other exchanges of this type been recorded in wars of the past? Of course the answer is yes, many times, and in one notable instance not very far from Bastogne, near the Belgian village of Waterloo.

Le Mot de Cambronne

Of the many legends that have grown out of the Battle of Waterloo, the most persistent is recounted with everything from admiration to ridicule. Here, for example, is a particularly reverent version of the event from one of the most outrageously partisan accounts available, John Abbott's two-volume epic of 1855, *The History of Napoleon Bonaparte*. The setting is the end of the day at the great battle. The climax has passed and the French have been routed. The charge of Napoleon's Old Guard has failed, and its remnants, comprising two battalions under General Pierre Cambronne, have drawn up a square in the French rear to cover the retreat of the Emperor.

> This invincible square, the last fragment of the Old Guard, nerved by that soul which its imperial creator had breathed into it, calmly closing up as death thinned its ranks, slowly and defiantly retired, arresting the flood of pursuit. General Cambronne was now bleeding from six wounds. But a few scores of men, torn and bleeding,

remained around him. The English and Prussians, admiring such heroism, and weary of the butchery, suspended for a moment their fire, and sent a flag of truce demanding a capitulation. General Cambronne returned the immortal reply, *"The Guard dies; it never surrenders!"* A few more volleys of bullets from the infantry, a few more discharges of grape-shot from the artillery, mowed them all down. Thus perished on the fatal field of Waterloo, the Old Guard of Napoleon. It was the creation of the genius of the Emperor; he had inspired it with his own lofty spirit; and the fall of the Emperor it devotedly refused to survive.

But Cambronne did not die there among his men, nor did he say any such thing. A more candid chronicler of the old school concedes the point, but insists that the attributed words epitomize what Cambronne *might* have said, "and in the phrase which seems to have been shouted by the men themselves in their last desperate struggle, they and their leader have found immortality."

What Cambronne *did* say, we now know, was *Merde!* (Shit!), and every schoolchild in France knows it too. In fact this word, which we can be assured was indeed shouted "by the men themselves in their last desperate struggle," assured the General's immortality more than any other act; the epithet is commonly and euphemistically known as *le mot de Cambronne* (the word of Cambronne). The loftier retort cited by Abbott (and the one that every schoolchild is officially taught) came from the pen of a Paris journalist years after the event.

Go Ahead, Make My Day!

In the history of warfare, *le mot de Cambronne* and *le mot de McAuliffe* are unquestionably two of the most celebrated ripostes on record. What they have in common is their ambiguity, a fact usually overlooked. Both are assumed to represent defiance rather than dismay, exasperation, or disgust, which are just as plausible. Beyond that their circumstances are very different. Cambronne's situation was hopeless, and his infamous word supports a myth of defiance in defeat. McAuliffe, it turned out, had the upper hand, and his response only strengthened it. But the defiance grew more emphatic in the retelling, as "the rest of the story" makes clear.

At Bastogne, the German emissaries, not surprisingly, were baffled by McAuliffe's reply. They expected the Americans to surrender. Not knowing precisely what *nuts* meant, they turned to Colonel Harper for some explanation. Years later, Harper recalled his response: "The reply is decidedly not affirmative, and if you continue this foolish attack, your losses will be tremendous." But apparently, while driving the Germans to the last outpost, Harper had second thoughts, and as he fumed over what he perceived as condescending arrogance on their part, he decided to elaborate on his answer in more emphatic terms. "If you don't understand what 'Nuts' means, in plain English it is the same as 'Go to hell.' I will tell you something else—if you continue to attack, we will kill every goddamn German that tries to break into this city." The ranking German officer saluted and said, "We will kill many Americans. This is war."

The exchange sounds too good to be true, as though it occurred to Harper much later what he ought to have said. In hindsight, he might as well have added, "Go ahead, make my day." At Bastogne, McAuliffe said what any tough customer would have under the circumstances; it might have been "Nuts!," or it could have been *le mot de Cambronne*. In either case, his irreverence perfectly countered the stereotype of German formality with good old American plain speaking. Harper's elaboration on the theme, on the other hand, strikes a false note.

The Birth of the "Nuts" Scenario

Voltaire, the prolific French philosophe and notorious misquoter, once noted that contrary to popular belief, history does not repeat itself, but historians do. The "nuts" episode is a great story (as is the story of *le mot de Cambronne*), but more than that it is a great *type* of story, one that has in fact been told many times in a variety of settings. Literary critics would call it a motif, one of the finite number of plots suitable for heroic narrative.

Probably not the first, but certainly one of the more influential "nuts" stories can be found in Herodotus, the Greek writer known as the Father of History, who also seems to be the father of the "nuts" scenario. The story concerns a tribe called the Scythians, a nomadic people who inhabited a region north of Thrace, just above the Dardanelles peninsula in modern-day Turkey and Bulgaria. In the sixth century BC, the Scythians incurred the disfavor of Darius the Great, the king of Persia, by daring to invade his possessions in Asia Minor. In return, Darius mustered a sizable force and marched them off to Scythia. Learning of this dire threat, the Scythian king Idanthyrsus appealed to his neighboring kings for help, but they declined. "You have brought this on yourselves," they said, "and we refuse to interfere." So Idanthyrsus and his men took to their horses and led Darius on a chase through neighboring lands, ravaging as they went. Frustrated by these unorthodox tactics, Darius sent an ultimatum to Idanthyrsus, which read:

> Strange man, why do you keep on flying before me, when there are two things you might do so easily? If you deem yourself able to resist my arms, cease your wanderings and come, let us engage in battle. Or if you are conscious that my strength is greater than yours—even so you should cease to run away—you have but to bring your lord earth and water, and come at once to a conference.

Earth and water were the traditional tokens of surrender, and Idanthyrsus had no intention of supplying them. Nor was he foolish enough to engage the Persians in open battle. So he sent his regrets, along with a two-word suggestion: "Go howl."

It is probably safe to say that stories of this sort had been floating around long before Herodotus decided to include this one in his *Histories.* Yet the Father of History seems to have missed its possibilities. At his next opportunity, in telling the tale of the defiant Leonidas and his celebrated last stand at Thermopylae, he failed to follow through, and the punch line had to be provided by Plutarch.

Come and Take Them

The story of Leonidas and the 300 Spartans is well-known as both a literary and a historical allusion. Its denouement is recounted at length in Chapter 10, but here is how it came about. In the year 480 BC, King Xerxes of Persia (the son of Darius the Great) set out with a combined army and navy of unprecedented magnitude to avenge the defeat his father had suffered ten years earlier at the Battle of Marathon. Like his father, Xerxes was overconfident; but even worse, he was arrogant. Warned by his inside man, the exiled Spartan king Demaratus, that the Greeks were formidable foes, the King was not impressed. When Demaratus further warned that the Spartans obeyed only one commandment, forbidding them to flee in battle, and either conquer or die whatever the number of the enemy, again Xerxes could only laugh.

The great King did not bother to send negotiators to Athens or Sparta. His father had done so ten years earlier, and the Athenians had thrown their heralds into a pit while the Spartans tossed theirs down a well, as if to say, "Here is where you will find your earth and your water" (a rather crude way of saying "nuts"). Instead Xerxes came with a force numbering over four million men (if we choose to believe Herodotus) and an ultimatum for the Spartans (if we choose to believe Plutarch), which read: "Hand over your arms." Leonidas, with characteristic Spartan bluntness, wrote back his now famous, in-your-face reply: "Come and take them."

Xerxes did take them, eventually, but not before an epic struggle that cost him thousands of men and held his invasion up long enough to cheat him of his best chance of victory. The Greeks soon thereafter drove the Persians out of their land with victories at Salamis and Plataea. As for the defiant words of Leonidas, they can be found on the pedestal of a statue of a Spartan hoplite that now stands guard over the pass, marking the event to which all last stands are inevitably compared.

Neither "Go howl" nor "Come and take them" became figures of speech, and Anthony McAuliffe probably never heard of them. But he most certainly knew of events in American history that could have supplied him with the verbal ammunition he needed. In the Mexican-American War, for example, General Zachary Taylor found himself hemmed in by a numerically superior force at Buena Vista when he received an ultimatum eerily similar to the one the Germans concocted at Bastogne. Its peculiar formality leads one to suspect that warfare had, since Xerxes' time, evolved an entire branch of etiquette that dictated such niceties as the proper wording of a surrender request. Here is the text of Santa Anna's note to Taylor, dated 22 February 1847:

> You are surrounded by twenty thousand men, and can not in any human probability avoid suffering a rout, and being cut to pieces with your troops; but as you deserve consideration and particular esteem, I wish to save you from a catastrophe, and for that purpose give you this notice, in order that you may surrender at discretion, under the assurance that you will be treated with the consideration belonging to the Mexican character; to which end you will be granted an hour's time to make up your mind, to commence from the moment when my flag of truce arrives in your camp. With this view I assure you of my particular consideration.

Taylor was not amused, and his reply has been enshrined in the annals of defiance along with McAuliffe's. "Tell him to go to hell!" he supposedly muttered, leaving it to his assistants to recast the sentiment in diplomatic terms suitable for delivery to the Mexican general. The story is believable enough, although it obscures a key point: Taylor must have suspected that Santa Anna was bluffing. The very wording of the surrender demand gives it away.

Far more famous than Taylor's gruff reply is John Paul Jones's response to the commander of the British frigate *Serapis*, when asked whether he was prepared to surrender his ship. As popular legend has it, Jones yelled back, "I have not yet begun to fight." The same thought probably ran through McAuliffe's mind at Bastogne, but he was not about to crib from the Marines. Still, the story is worth a closer look.

There's a Shot in the Locker

The clash between Jones's *Bonhomme Richard* and the *Serapis* occurred off Flamborough Head, part of England's Yorkshire coast, on 25 September 1779, during the American War of Independence. With a small squadron of three ships, Jones had been plaguing British shipping routes for weeks, trying to disrupt the supply of much-needed coal bound for London. Early on the morning of the 25th, he found what he was looking for: a convoy of 39 ships coming around Flamborough Head escorted by two warships. One of these was the *Serapis*, a 44-gun frigate commanded by Captain Richard Pearson. Not only did the *Serapis* pack more firepower than Jones's *Bonhomme Richard*, but its copper hull made it faster and more maneuverable. All in all, Pearson enjoyed a 3 to 2 tactical advantage over Jones. To make matters worse, when the two ships closed, two of Jones's largest guns, his eighteen-pounders, exploded, killing their gun crews. The other gunners then refused to fire the large cannons, fearing they were all defective. With Jones's artillery strength now reduced by about a third, Pearson's

138

advantage in firepower increased to 2 to 1 before the duel was barely under way.

Few ships have gone into battle with such a handicap and survived, and Jones realized that he could not long withstand the British cannon fire. His only chance was to lock horns with the enemy and try to board their ship with his French marines. But by the time Jones managed to grapple onto the *Serapis*, the pounding from its guns had rent his hull and the *Bonhomme Richard* was taking on water. Its flag had been shot off and trailed in the ship's wake. Perhaps mistaking this for a signal of surrender, Captain Pearson called out, "Has your ship struck?" (meaning had they struck the colors), to which Jones gave his famous reply that he had not yet begun to fight. Jones's own first lieutenant, Richard Dale, later remarked, "I am positive that no American or Irish officer had any more notion of quitting than Jones himself had."

In the eighteenth century, sailors had a saying—"Never say die when there's a shot in the locker"—a point that could be taken too literally. At the Battle of the Nile in 1798, the French admiral Blanquet du Chayla, like Jones, fought off British attackers on deck alongside his men until his ship, *Le Franklin*, was nearly incapacitated. Severely wounded, Blanquet revived after his crew stopped firing and struck the flag. Upon being informed that only three of his guns were still operational, he replied, "Never mind, go on firing. The last shot may bring victory." It did not. The French fleet was overwhelmed by the superior tactics of Horatio Nelson.

At Flamborough Head, John Paul Jones, unlike Blanquet, had more than one shot left in the locker, and a shipload of tough, like-minded sailors. According to Dale:

> Just as Jones retorted to Pearson that he "hadn't begun to fight," he noticed old Jack Robinson right at his elbow and, in the way of jolly banter he always had in battle, sang out to him: "Hey! Jack! old trump! What say you to quitting?" To which old Jack quickly

answered in his low growl, "There's a shot left in the locker, sir!"

After closing with the *Serapis* and directing his men to grapple onto her, Jones arrayed his sharpshooters on deck, in the rigging, and out on the yardarms to keep the British from cutting the ropes that bound the ships' fates while sustaining the Americans' only hope. Jones had all but abandoned his cannon and relied on musket fire to keep the British sailors below decks, where they continued to pound away from point-blank range with their eighteen-pounders. As the *Bonhomme Richard* slowly disintegrated under the barrage, American and French sailors wreaked havoc on the *Serapis*, culminating with the detonation of some powder cartridges that the British powder boys had dumped within reach of an open hatch. The explosion killed some twenty men and gave Jones the idea of trying to bring down the ship's mainmast with his few functioning guns. When Pearson, seeing that the *Bonhomme Richard* was sinking, again asked Jones if he wished to ask for quarter, Jones replied, "No, sir, I haven't as yet *thought* of it, but I'm determined to make *you* strike." Some naval chroniclers place his more famous words here.

The fight went on for three and a half hours, at which point half of Jones's crew had been killed or wounded; his ship was on fire, had five feet of water in its hold, and it was taking on more each moment. His quarterdeck was about to collapse into the gun room, his main deck was about to fall into the hold, and his rigging was a shambles. Yet he continued the fight alongside his men for another half hour, at which point Captain Pearson, whose own ship and crew had reached the point of desperation, struck the British flag and offered Jones his sword. As Jones accepted it, the mainmast of the *Serapis* toppled into the sea.

The U.S. Marines look to this fight as a source of their pride and the measure of their worth, and they would need such inspiration. During the Second World War, they proved their worth yet again, giving rise to another legend of gallant defiance, this time at Wake Island. Of course, there is more to the story than meets the eye.

Send More Japs

The legend of Wake Island is best understood as an instance of wishful misinterpretation. An American garrison of 400 Marines stationed on the central Pacific island in the days after the Japanese attack on Pearl Harbor waited for the inevitable with no hope of reinforcement. The Japanese navy was now unopposed, yet the garrison at Wake had more than a few shots left in the locker. During the initial Japanese assault they played possum and lured several enemy destroyers within lethal range, and then opened fire from their shore batteries. They sunk two of the ships. Although their initial success was heartening, the end result was inevitable. But back at home, the story played out as one of intrepid defiance, with comparisons to the Alamo and Thermopylae. As rumor had it, the signalman at Wake contacted Pearl Harbor with the message: "Send us more Japs."

The heroes themselves were quick to deny it. According to James P. S. Devereaux, deputy commander of the 400 Marines at Wake, "That was news to me." Claiming to speak for every man on the island, he said, "Anybody that wants it can sure have my share of the Japs we already got. In any case," he added, "I would not have been damn fool enough to send such an idiotic message." But the denials came too late. The story made the rounds and gave Americans something to cheer about after the horrific events at Pearl. Wake Island would soon capitulate, but not before the legend of its sixteen-day holdout set the tone for the battle of the Pacific.

The most plausible explanation for the message, issued by U.S. Navy Commander W. Scott Cunningham, the ranking officer at Wake, states that after the Marines had beaten back the attack, the signalman coded and reported the incident. Following standard procedure, he padded the message with some nonsense tacked onto the beginning. Its essential meaning was "Send help," but the message was perhaps too cleverly disguised. It read: SEND US STOP NOW IS THE TIME FOR ALL GOOD MEN TO COME TO THE AID OF THEIR PARTY STOP CUNNINGHAM STOP MORE JAPS. Someone on the receiving end apparently pieced together the opening and closing words, and the legend was off and running. But as Cunningham later explained:

> What the world took as a gesture of defiant heroism from Wake Island was nothing of the kind and was never intended to be. In fact, those of us on Wake realized as the days passed, the whole idea of heroism can be tremendously, even embarrassingly, misleading. The picture conjured up by the radio reports was as far removed from reality as Wake was from Pearl Harbor. And this, in a way, was inevitable; no man can completely understand what war is like until he has experienced it for himself.

Here Cunningham hits at a larger truth than he may have realized. No one can entirely control a legend, not even the subject of it. After the humiliation of Pearl Harbor, Americans at home yearned for gestures of defiance. The defenders of Wake may have wanted no part of the story, but the fact is that while it was *about* them, it was not *for* them. They didn't need it, but the American people did. "We were doing our best," wrote Cunningham, "and we were proud of it, but our best seldom included that disregard for sanity that marks so many romantic visions of the thin red line of heroes." The thin red line, in this case, connects Leonidas at Thermopylae with Horatius at the bridge, with Roland (of *The Song of Roland*) at Roncevalles, with John Paul Jones at Flamborough Head—all instances in which the situation looked grim. In December of 1941, every American home tuned into the war, either through newspapers and magazines or through newsreels or radio broadcasts. The media brought each reader and listener to Wake, so that they too could stare down the overwhelming might of the Japanese navy. SEND MORE JAPS spoke for these vicarious participants, and boosted morale where it was needed.

The Marine garrison at Wake Island held out for as long as it could against an overwhelming force, and then surrendered. The patriotic film version released the following year omitted this detail, and instead portrayed it as a Thermopylae or Alamo; it ends with the actors digging in and fighting to the last man. For some reason (and it can't have been fidelity to the truth), the filmmakers omitted the Send More Japs episode entirely.

Contempt for the Enemy

Defiance plays out as one of the most useful and perhaps most underrated elements of military strategy. It can take the sting out of a defeat or give hope to the hopeless by showing contempt for the enemy. In some cases a small spiritual victory may lead to a real one in the war itself, as it ultimately did at Wake, at the Alamo, and at Thermopylae.

On the other hand, passive acceptance may sometimes be the wiser course, although it can carry a psychological burden. To this day, many citizens of Prague agonize over their failure to stand up to the Soviet clampdown during the Prague Spring of 1968. As Bruce Rosenberg notes in *Custer and the Epic of Defeat*, much of the Czechs' resentment was directed at Alexander Dubcek, the Czech Communist Party leader who pushed for passive capitulation to the Russian army.

> When I asked [a hotel owner] what the Czechs might have done against so strong an invading force . . . he said, "We might have fought. Even if only for a half an hour. At least we should have done *something*."

The nineteenth-century essayist and orator George William Curtis once noted that every great crisis of human history is a pass of Thermopylae, "and there is always a Leonidas and his three hundred to die in it, if they cannot conquer." Perhaps, but there is not always a Herodotus or a Plutarch to immortalize the deed. Many Czechs did do something. At least a dozen died trying to defend the Prague radio building. What they lacked was an indelible image to capture their resolve—something like the lone student who stood up to the Chinese tanks at Tiananmen Square.

Yet even when the world does take note, it sometimes is not impressed. There must be something irreproachably worthwhile at stake. Hardly anyone remembers the Scythians, however much they may have impressed Herodotus. Few Americans care to recall Zachary Taylor with the same awe they reserve for John Paul Jones or General McAuliffe. The Mexican-American War was viewed in many quarters as a shameless act of imperial aggression. Its legend-building apparatus was soon dismantled and was reassembled only after the outbreak of the Civil War.

Then there is "the rest of the story." With all of this ado about defiance, we sometimes forget to ask how it all turned out. The defenders of Wake Island held out bravely, but only for a few weeks. With reinforcement impossible, Japanese bombing finally overwhelmed them, and the garrison was forced to surrender. Transported to Japanese prisons, they would not be liberated until the end of the war. The Scythians ultimately wore the Persians down and drove them back into Asia. Leonidas' 300 held out for six days, but in the end were overwhelmed by Xerxes' army. At Buena Vista, Santa Anna had not been bluffing about outnumbering the Americans, although he had been trying to bluff his way out of having to fight. His army of 20,000 had marched 45 miles in less than a day with little food, water, or rest, and probably numbered no more than 15,000 not-very-effective troops by the time they reached the battlefield. An American force of less than 5000 prevailed in a well-contested fight, but Taylor got very little mileage out of his act of defiance. Viewed by many Americans as unjustified and unprincipled, the Mexican-American War produced no popular legends. Far more celebrated than Taylor's refusal to surrender was his order to Captain Braxton Bragg at the height of the battle, which is given by some writers as, "A little more grape, Captain Bragg," and by others as, "Double-shot your guns and give 'em hell!"

As for Pierre Cambronne of Napoleon's Old Guard, he passed up his only chance to surrender. Struck a glancing blow to the forehead by a spent musket ball, he was knocked out. Battlefield scavengers stripped him naked, and he was eventually taken prisoner to England. Although court-martialed for treason and sentenced to death on his return to France, Cambronne appealed his sentence and received a pardon from the restored King Louis XVIII. He married an Englishwoman.

Finally, to tie up the last loose end, the relief of Bastogne came quickly. Luettwitz could not effectively carry out his threat to wipe out the encircled U.S. troops. The allies air-dropped desperately needed supplies, and by Christmas Day Patton's 4th Armored Division rolled through the southern end of the "bulge." The German counteroffensive had stalled and, although the battle raged on for many more weeks, Bastogne became the symbol of German failure and American persistence.

If

The account of the "Nuts" incident given above is drawn in large part from John Eisenhower's very thorough history of the Battle of the Bulge (*The Bitter Woods*). To confirm the story, Eisenhower contacted both McAuliffe and Harper in 1966. Neither man had any incentive to refute the official record. They had not been conscious of making history at the time, and when they found that by doing a difficult job the best way they knew how they had become heroes, they dutifully climbed onto the bandwagon. If the story required some polishing up for public consumption, so be it. In this case the polishing was probably done by McAuliffe's superiors. Specifically, Lieutenant General Omar Bradley, commander of the 12th Army Group in Luxembourg, had begun vetting quotes from his generals by the time of the Ardennes offensive. Stung by George Patton's embarrassing frankness with the press, Bradley had ordered the censors "not to pass any direct quotes from *any* commander without my approval." After the relief of Bastogne, Bradley remembers being called to the phone and told, "We've got a direct quote from General McAuliffe. Do you want us to pass it?"

"What did he say?" asked Bradley.

"Nuts," came the reply.

Or something to that effect. The consensus now seems to be that what McAuliffe really said and wrote was "Balls!," which helps to explain the confusion on the part of the Germans.

Whatever McAuliffe said, it was terse enough to earn him the fitting sobriquet of the "laconic general." Fitting because that term, which describes a distaste for fine words and verbosity, comes from Laconia (or Lacedaemon), the home of that most laconic of all peoples, the Spartans. Next to them, even McAuliffe seems like a windbag, if we are to believe this story, another unsubstantiated bit of legend that comes to us via Plutarch:

When Philip of Macedon wrote a threatening letter to the Spartans, warning: "If I enter Lacedaemon, I shall raze it," they wrote back a one-word reply: "If."

Thou shalt save alive nothing that breatheth.

Deuteronomy

You won't surrender, eh! Fire away then, and fight your best; for if I catch you, you shall get no quarter.

An Abenaki chief
Massacre at Fort William Henry (French and Indian War)
9 August 1757

Nothing will disorganize an army more or ruin it more completely than pillage.

Napoleon
Maxims

We give express charge that in our marches through the country there be nothing compelled from the villages, nothing taken but paid for, none of the French upbraided or abused in disdainful language; for when lenity and cruelty play for a kingdom, the gentler gamester is soonest the winner.

Shakespeare's *Henry V* in France

147

A medieval city under siege. From a 15th century illuminated manuscript.

CHAPTER NINE

Cry Havoc!

LETTING SLIP THE DOGS OF WAR AT HARFLEUR AND FORT WILLIAM HENRY

Harfleur

For five weeks in the late summer of 1415, England's King Henry V besieged the French city of Harfleur, bombarding it with artillery fire, digging mines beneath its walls, and in all losing some 2000 men in a typically slow war of attrition which, in this instance, began to tip the balance in favor of the besieged. The incident might have faded into obscurity like countless other sieges had it not been dramatized by William Shakespeare, who marked the event with one of the most stirring pieces of oratory in English history. Its opening line refers to a breach in the city wall opened up through the efforts of the king's siege engineer, Master Giles, a specialist in the new science of artillery fire. After the English failed to dig their way under the walls, Henry turned to Giles, who bombarded one gate relentlessly, creating the gap that set the stage for the famous words:

> Once more into the breach, dear friends, once more,
> or close up the wall with our English dead.

Rousing words, to be sure, but as the ensuing harangue goes on—and on—a distinct tone of frustration, exasperation, and even desperation sets in. King Henry is doggedly trying to take back what he believes to be rightfully his, and he has been at it quite a while. The summer is about to end with nothing to

149

show for it except men who are falling victim to boredom, to lethargy and, worst of all, to dysentery. By the time the speech winds down to a close accumulated frustrations have risen to the surface; the words *once more* echo with grating insistence as Henry calls forth one demand on body or soul on top of another: "Stiffen the sinews, conjure up the blood . . . set the teeth, stretch the nostril wide, hold hard the breath . . . bend up every spirit . . . dishonor not your mothers." Little wonder that when the town finally relents, the English are so weary of war, so doubtful of the prospect of sacking another town, and so sick of fighting, sick with fever, and sick of the French, that they pull out and advance more or less "to the rear," back to the English stronghold of Calais. Along the way, of course, they will march into a trap set for them at Agincourt by a French force many times their size.

Henry's relentless assault on Harfleur involved more than artillery and siege craft. In the play he also resorts to some threats that seem extreme under the circumstances. Close on the heels of the "once more into the breach" episode, he warns the governor of the town that if Harfleur does not surrender, he will capture it anyway and turn his men loose on its women and children, a threat he embellishes with the appalling image of "the flesh'd soldier, rough and hard of heart, in liberty of bloody hand . . . rang[ing] with conscience wide as hell, mowing like grass, your fresh faced virgins and your flowering infants." This speech, it should be noted, is purely a playwright's invention and not historical fact (as far as we know). But Shakespeare was not making it up entirely. The threat was frighteningly believable in wars of that era, which raises the question of why Henry or any king would go to such lengths merely to take a town. Was he prepared to make good on his terrifying threat, and what would the consequences be if he did? Of course the town relents, leaving one to wonder what sort of fellow this Henry is.

The issue is further complicated by another scene in the play, one also based on a true incident, in which Shakespeare reveals the king to be a man of principle even when it costs him personally. When petitioned to rescind the death sentence imposed on his former drinking companion Bardolf, who has been caught pilfering a trifle from a church, he refuses, explaining:

> We would have all such offenders so cut off: and we give express charge that in our marches through the country there be nothing compelled from the villages, nothing taken but paid for, none of the French upbraided or abused in disdainful language; for when lenity and cruelty play for a kingdom, the gentler gamester is soonest the winner.

For his seemingly petty theft, Bardolf is strung up from a tree.

How are we to reconcile this enlightened and considerate policy toward the villagers with the king's appalling threats at Harfleur? To a modern audience it may seem baffling, but Shakespeare's audience would have had no trouble reconciling the two Henrys. What we tend to forget is that Henry V could be magnanimous in the field and unscrupulous to the inhabitants of a walled town because the laws of war not only allowed it, but demanded it. As painful as the decision to execute Bardolf may have been, it was also a pragmatic one. Nothing destroys discipline within an army as effectively as pillaging. Such acts had to be dealt with swiftly and severely. Consideration for civilians had little to do with it. As for his behavior at Hartfleur, King Henry was merely following the standard practice of his day (if not of Shakespeare's day), which, also for pragmatic reasons, happened to be particularly brutal with respect to sieges.

The Nasty Business of Siege Craft

Sieges cannot compete with battles for drama, but they loom so much larger in the history of warfare, both in number and tactical importance, that they demanded a different set of rules that were far less chivalrous than those that applied on the battlefield. This begins to explain why the laws of war from Biblical times until surprisingly recent times have dealt so harshly with the citizens of besieged towns. In this respect Shakespeare stayed close to the historical record, and his audience would have understood much better than a modern audience what was at stake at Harfleur. The siege was, in fact, of far greater consequence than Henry's stunning upset victory at Agincourt.

Although Henry V waged war by the rules, he knew quite well what those rules allowed him to do in the eyes of God and the Church. In a letter to the French King Charles V justifying his invasion, he asserted that "the law of Deuteronomy commands that whoever appears in arms before a town should offer it peace before it is besieged." And if it doesn't open its gates? According to Deuteronomy:

> [If a city] makes no peace with you, but makes war against you, you shall besiege it; and when the Lord your God gives it into your hand you shall put all its males to the sword, but . . . everything else in the city, all its spoils you shall take for yourselves.

This applied only to "distant cities." Regarding cities within Israel itself the law is unequivocal: "Thou shalt save alive nothing that breatheth." This is the fate that befell Jericho in 1350 BC, when Joshua and his Israelites "utterly destroyed all that was in the city, both man and woman, young and old, and ox, and sheep, and ass, with the edge of the sword."

The harshness of this rule of war, at least in the Bible, arose out of a desire for religious purity that was of paramount importance in ancient times. It was thought to be not merely expedient, but necessary. In time the necessity disappeared, yet the religious justification for the harsh treatment of besieged populations, as Henry V demonstrated, remained in full force. The reason that a Christian king would bypass the lessons of the Gospels in favor of the severe law of the Old Testament was a simple one: real estate was too important an investment.

This point is yet another of the great misconceptions of popular history, a misconception fostered by the "decisive battles" school of historians. Warfare through the ages has consisted mostly of sieges, skirmishes, and raids, with relatively few pitched battles. Furthermore, the pitched battles were far less important than the sieges. This explains why Sir Edward Creasy (in *Fifteen Decisive Battles of the World*, his best-seller of 1851) could identify only a handful of battles that qualified as both "decisive" and "of enduring importance." Of the fifteen he did focus on, several are in fact sieges rather than battles. Agincourt doesn't make the cut. Not only was it of far less consequence than the capture of Harfleur, but it was one of only four major pitched battles fought during the entire Hundred Years' War. (The others were Crécy in 1346, Poitiers in 1356, and Nájera in 1367.) None were particularly important for anything more than bragging rights. In each case the French initiated the fighting, deluded by their numerical superiority, and each time they lost. Yet in the end they won the war.

Henry's frustration at the walls of Harfleur went hand in hand with his understanding that only by obtaining supply centers and safe havens could an invading force hope to conquer. Open-field battles may have been glorious, but because they did not decide very much, both sides could afford to treat them almost like games, with comparatively lenient rules of engagement. Unless the battle turned into a massacre (and even when it did), all that was at stake was the field itself, which would soon be reclaimed by cattle or wheat. What really mattered was the acquisition of real estate, meaning cities and citadels, and the resettlement or elimination of their populations. By focusing on the chivalrous aspects of battle, history has misled us into thinking that sieges were barbaric deviations from the etiquette of combat, when in fact they followed a highly codified ethic. It just happened to be an ethic of appalling severity.

The Massacre at Fort William Henry

A good illustration of the delicate practice of siege and plunder occurred during the French and Indian War of 1754–1763, which pitted the French and certain northern Indian tribes against the British and their colonists for control of North America. In a particularly notorious incident made most famous, perhaps, by James Fennimore Cooper in *The Last of the Mohicans*, the Marquis de Montcalm, commanding the French forces, lost control of his Indian allies at Fort William Henry in New York. Admittedly, much of what we know of that war and of that particular incident comes to us from the nineteenth-century American historian Francis Parkman, whose *Montcalm and Wolfe* chronicles the fates of the opposing commanders, both of whom would die two years later at the Battle of Quebec. Their deaths led Parkman to idealize them to some extent. In his account of the Fort William Henry incident, for example, Parkman is careful to portray Montcalm as a gentleman, his Canadian allies as unreliable thugs, and the Indians as out-and-out savages enraged by an insatiable thirst for alcohol and blood. Because Parkman relied so heavily on contemporary journals, especially that of Montcalm's adjutant, Louis de Bouganville, his account undoubtedly presents as fact many of the prevalent prejudices of the day.

According to Parkman, in August of 1757 Montcalm led an army of about 7600 men, of which 1600 were Indians, on an expedition to capture Fort William Henry at the head of New York's Lake George. The fort, a wooden palisaded structure commanded by Lieutenant Colonel George Munro, housed a garrison of some 1600 English and colonial troops and a small artillery battery. Knowing that he could not hold out for very long against a siege, Munro had appealed for reinforcements to his superior, General Webb, who commanded a nearby garrison at Fort Edward. But Webb feared for his own security and, while he promised some support, he delivered hardly any. Munro and his men were essentially on their own.

154

Although three and a half centuries had passed since Agincourt, the English and French still observed the laws of war that had been in place at the time of Henry V. They tended to bend the rules from time to time, but tried not to break them. Thus when the firing at Fort William Henry began on August 4, Montcalm became concerned about the increasingly unruly behavior of his native allies. Needing their tactical support and relying on their knowledge of the local terrain, he had entered into a dangerous pact with the chiefs of the Six Nations. At the same time he was aware that, as he himself put it, these men were "lured by the prospect of gifts, scalps, and plunder." Thus Montcalm bowed to expedience and hoped for the best. But as his confidence of success grew, so did his apprehension. He knew that the Indians did not understand the finer points of a just war, prompting him to send this message to Munro:

> I owe it to humanity to summon you to surrender. At present I can restrain the savages, and make them observe the terms of a capitulation, as I might not have the power to do under other circumstances; and an obstinate defense on your part could only retard the capture of the place a few days, and endanger an unfortunate garrison which cannot be relieved, in consequence of the dispositions I have made. I demand a decisive answer within an hour.

Of course, to our ears this sounds suspiciously like General Luettwitz's ultimatum at Bastogne or Santa Anna's at Buena Vista, if not Henry V's at Harfleur, leading us to suspect that Montcalm could indeed control his men and was merely putting to good use the fearsome reputation of the "savages"— a reputation he himself had helped to perpetuate. Not surprisingly, Munro rejected the request and expressed his resolve to fight it out. (Unfortunately, we do not have the exact words he used.) In what seems like yet another bit of Herodotan literary

155

license, Parkman foreshadows the outcome by passing on the unlikely remark of an Abenaki chief, who, learning of Munro's defiance, said, "You won't surrender, eh! Fire away then, and fight your best; for if I catch you, you shall get no quarter."

After five days of artillery pounding, Munro began to run out of options. He had lost more than 300 of his men, most of his guns had failed, and to make matters worse, smallpox was raging through the fort. With no prospect of reinforcement, he acceded to a negotiated surrender according him the following generous terms: the English would be allowed to march out with honors of war and be escorted to Fort Edward, they would agree not to serve against the French for a period of 18 months, all French prisoners would be released, and the English would be allowed to retain one field piece in recognition of a brave resistance.

The Indian chiefs also signed off on this agreement, promising to restrain their young warriors. But such a gracious settlement was not going to work out. The Indians plundered the fort as soon as the soldiers had evacuated it, slaughtering many of the sick and wounded. Then they began to harass the English encampment, looking for rum. The French guard "could not or would not keep out the rabble," as Parkman describes it, and as the Indians rummaged through the English camp throughout the afternoon, Montcalm rushed to the scene to try to restore the peace. According to Bouganville, "The Marquis spared no efforts to prevent the rapacity of the savages and, I must say, of certain persons associated with them, from resulting in something worse than plunder." The persons he refers to are undoubtedly the Canadians, whose officers Montcalm had placed in charge of the escort.

Bouganville was not present the next day when the English column marched out, but he filed the following report, which puts the best possible spin on Montcalm's actions:

> At daybreak the English, who were inconceivably frightened by the sight of the Indians, wished to leave

before our escort was all assembled and in place. They abandoned their trunks and other heavy baggage . . . and started to march. The Indians had already butchered a few sick in the tents which served as a hospital. The Abenakis . . . commenced the riot. They shouted the death cry and hurled themselves on the tail of the column which started to march out. The English, instead of showing resolution, were seized with fear and fled in confusion, throwing away their arms, their baggage, and even their coats. Their fear emboldened the Indians of all nations who started pillaging, killed some dozen soldiers, and took away five or six hundred. Our escort did what it could. A few [French] grenadiers were wounded. The Marquis de Montcalm rushed up at the noise; M. de Bourlamaque and several French officers risked their lives tearing the English from the hands of the Indians. For in a case like this the Indians respect nothing. . . . Finally the disorder quieted down and the Marquis de Montcalm at once took away from the Indians four hundred of these unfortunate men and had them clothed. The French officers divided with the English officers the few spare clothes they had, and the Indians, loaded with booty, disappeared the same day.

Parkman presents eyewitness testimony from both the French and English sides and, not surprisingly, it weighs heaviest against the Indians. His estimates are unreliable, but subsequent research has placed the number killed at 69 at the least, and 185 at the most. Out of the 2300 who surrendered (a figure that includes about 700 civilians), 286 never returned. The French did their best to recover most of the captives, and after reassembling the English column they marched them off to Fort Edward under heavy guard.

In the so-called Massacre at William Henry, the Marquis de Montcalm nearly let his command spiral downward into total war. To the extent that Parkman can be believed (and it should be kept in mind that he wanted nothing to detract from Montcalm's heroic death at the Battle of Quebec), the French general appears to have momentarily stumbled into the heart of darkness, and then recovered his footing. But he could not make everything right. The American press had a field day, calling for the British side to lash back in kind. They didn't, at least as a matter of policy. Atrocities continued to occur in remote places, but the British had centuries of experience fighting the French, and they reserved their vengeance (as did the colonists once they had gained independence) for the Indians. Lord Jeffrey Amherst, who later became the British Major General in America, used the massacre as an excuse for denying any of the courtesies of war to the natives, and European-Americans would carry on this tradition with the same vengeance after America won its independence. But even as they made their way northward in the wake of the massacre, the Indians carried an even faster-germinating seed of their own suffering. Unbeknownst to them, along with the prisoners they took back to Canada, they carried a devastating epidemic of smallpox.

The Ultimate Victims of Sieges

History serves up countless instances of means that justify ends, but hardly glorify them. More than any other act of war, sieges have given rise to the worst forms of atrocities, particularly against civilians. Yet such acts have always been "justified" after the fact by the circumstances. One Jericho, it was thought, could make enough of an impression on a populace to encourage other towns to surrender without a fight. This could save an invader such a prodigious effort that the threat seemed worth making, and occasionally carrying out. It also explains why if a city resisted, its inhabitants could expect something like a reenactment of the fall of Troy.

On the other hand, some invaders would punish a city that *failed* to put up a noble resistance, while rewarding those that did. Montcalm, in a siege at Oswego prior to the taking of Fort William Henry, had refused to extend any honors to the garrison because, by his own estimation, they had mounted such a poor defense. He took them all prisoner. At Fort William Henry the Indians held to a more biblical idea: that any city taken by force had no recourse to laws of war, laws of nature, or laws of God. Women could be raped, men tortured and killed, children slaughtered or enslaved, properties seized or destroyed, and all quite justifiably. This is what European warfare had taught them. The Marquis de Montcalm led them to believe that they would have their biblical revenge, and when denied it, they rebelled.

What the Indians did not know was that in practice, the ransacking of a town in the late middle ages constituted a ritualistic set piece—not a spontaneous orgy, but a deliberate and methodical act. The battle cry "havoc," which had far more dire implications than the word carries today, had by Henry V's era been banned. In *The Laws of War in the Middle Ages*, Oxford historian M.H. Keen concedes that sometimes the sack of a town got out of control, but looting and ransacking did not typically give way to havoc, nor were they carried out in the heat of battle. So common was the practice of dividing up the spoils, in fact, and so much did the average soldier depend on it for his income, that even by the 1200s it had become systematized, with spoils being carefully allotted according to rank. According to Keen:

> The word "assault" must not be allowed to convey the impression that these excesses, lawfully permitted in a conquered town, were necessarily committed in hot blood. All that "assault" meant was that surrender was unconditional. Thus, when Calais capitulated in 1347, the men of the garrison marched out bareheaded with naked swords in their hands, and the burgesses with

halters about their necks; this was a sign that even though it had not been stormed, Edward III had taken the town by force of arms unconditionally, and that the lives of those in it were at his mercy. He could take his time to decide their fate, if he wished. In a similar way, when Luxembourg was taken by the Burgundians in 1463, it was not sacked forthwith. The troops remained with their standards until after Philip the Good had entered the conquered town, and had been to the Church of Notre Dame to pray and give thanks. Then, and only then, the word was given, and the whole town systematically plundered from one end to the other.

Keen goes on to explain that, cold-blooded as this may sound, it was considered nothing more than a standard operating procedure. The captured town was literally at the king's pleasure, and while he sometimes might allow an uncontrolled pillage as a reward for his men, he was more likely to order a careful division of the spoils—a dispensing of justice rather than an act of war.

The losers in all such incidents were the civilian populations. Caught between a garrison that would be punished if it did not resist and a besieger who threatened worse punishments if they did, the citizens of besieged cities became helpless pawns, unprotected by any of the rules of war, and thus at the mercy not only of the besieger but of the garrison defending their city. At the siege of Calais in 1346, which lasted a full year, King Edward III allowed 1700 civilians to leave the city and even supplied them with food and money. Later, when 500 more sought to leave, he barred their way, condemning them to starve to death in the no-man's land between the city walls and the English lines. The citizens of Harfleur were spared this only because the siege ended before food stores dwindled. But two years later, at the six-month siege of Rouen in 1418, scarcity of food forced the garrison to expel the citizenry. To maintain pressure on the French, Henry V refused to allow the civilians to pass through his lines, forcing them to spend the winter in the broad ditch surrounding the walls of the city. Poorly clothed and barely fed, thousands of them died under Henry's impassive gaze.

It is only natural to judge the past in terms of the present and to overlook the prevailing mores, folkways, and conditions of distant times, places, and peoples. To the undiscriminating moralist this may sound like a rationalization, but to ignore it can lead to some dangerously misguided assertions. For example, recently a prominent journalist profiling a new production of *Henry V* took aim at one scene in the play (and a real incident of the war) that is usually underplayed or edited out, although this production intended to highlight it. The scene takes place at the height of the Battle of Agincourt, at a moment when Henry senses that his victory might be snatched away. After being informed that his baggage train has been attacked (by the local villagers, it turned out), he gives an order to kill the French prisoners. Appalled at such a flagrant violation of the conventions of war, his knights refuse, and the task falls to the bowmen, who, like Montcalm's Indians, had no qualms about it. With the victory firmly in hand, Henry rescinds the order, but not before an unknown number of French knights have been slaughtered. The journalist referred to this as "an atrocity on a scale of horror almost unimaginable, even by contemporary standards." It is the kind of statement that shows a want of imagination, a failure to appreciate the practice of war in the Middle Ages, or both.

To the knights who refused to carry out the order, the horror consisted of losing a king's ransom. To the French themselves it was easily imaginable: before the battle they had promised to give no quarter to the English, and had threatened to cut the hands off the longbowmen. Besides, prisoners taken during a battle could not expect good treatment when they became a burden or a threat to their captors. As for sug-

gesting that atrocities can be ranked, the sad truth is that anyone familiar with war in the twentieth century can imagine a
far broader scale of horror than anything that was on display
at Agincourt.

Perhaps what the journalist found appalling was the
idea that the fictional Henry, as played sympathetically by
Lawrence Olivier or Kenneth Branagh, would contemplate
such a dastardly thing, much less allow it. But both Olivier
and Branagh, to the relief of many, left the scene out of
their filmed versions of the play. Left out altogether, not
only from the play but from the pages of history, is the
plight of those who suffered the most in the wars of
Europe—the noncombatants.

I grieve, not because I have to die for my country, but only because I have not lifted my arm against the enemy, or done any deed worthy of me, much as I have desired to achieve something.

Callicrates
At the Battle of Plataea
479 BC
Herodotus, *Histories*

My regret is to be struck in this way, without having been able to lead my regiment on the enemy.

Charles Ardant du Picq
At Longeville-les-Metz
Franco-Prussian War
1870

The Battle of Plataea, 479 BC.

CHAPTER TEN

You Were Not There!

OPPORTUNITIES WON AND LOST

Brave Crillon

In his *Henriade*, an epic poem inspired by the tumultuous military career of Henry IV of France, the prolific French writer Voltaire reproduces a letter written by the king to one of his field marshals, Louis de Bertons, Lord of Crillon, shortly before an engagement at Amiens. The details of time and place are unimportant; Voltaire alters them to suit a greater purpose, which is to display a distinctly French form of affectionate ridicule. In the poem's most famous line, the king takes his officer to task for missing his most recent victory:

> Hang yourself, brave Crillon; we fought at Arques and
> you were not there. But I love you all the same.

The line has since gained a measure of infamy. It now graces a plaque on the Hotel Crillon near the Place de la Concorde in Paris, and has attached itself just as securely to poor Crillon's reputation.

Crillon was no shirker. He has been called the Ney of his era, a flattering reference to one of Napoleon's most dashing generals, who, while sometimes late to the battlefield, was always there. But Crillon was not at Arques, and though he would live on to fight another day, the king's playful message rings clearly: "You may be a brave chap, or some may call you brave, and of course you really are a most gallant fellow, my dear Crillon, yet when we took on 20,000 of the enemy with a mere 9,000 of our own at Arques, you were not there. You missed it."

Everyone can appreciate the agony of a missed opportunity, but few of us are likely to lose any sleep over missing out on a chance to be disemboweled, emasculated, beheaded, blown to pieces, maimed for life, or simply killed outright by an arquebus shot to the brainpan. The degree of carnage wrought by war in the twentieth century has taken much of the gloss off of romantic notions of battle. Even so, the idea of battle as the quintessential and most honorable form of human struggle persists for many people. This is because while war is understood to be a nasty business, it does hold out a chance for glory if one merely lives through it. In even the most Pyrrhic bloodbaths, fate bestows the victory on a few, and blesses them with either superficial wounds or no wounds at all. Even those who die, whether they die nobly or ignominiously, are immortalized in such inspiring tributes as Pericles' funeral oration (for those who died serving Athens in the first years of the Peloponnesian War) or Lincoln's Gettysburg Address. In fact, while the overt message of any war memorial is that the men listed below were there, the subliminal message is that *you* were not. They died so that you might visit and reflect upon their monument.

This gives rise to an inevitable and unavoidable theme in military history writing which asserts that battle is a rite of passage open to a select few, who are thereby set apart from the many. In some cultures it has been regarded as the most important rite of all, with the result that the fear of missing out can exceed the fear of war itself. Lost in this idealization is any sense of what happens in battle and what price has to be paid. This can have unfortunate consequences.

The History of Nations Is the History of Their Armies

Any war literature worth reading, whether fictional or historical, inevitably makes the case that battles, sieges, and raids, from full-scale invasions down to the most incidental skirmishes, are the only subjects worthy of our attention or admiration. The hero may learn some sobering lessons and witness horrors that will haunt him forever, but he can truly claim to have confronted life's deepest questions and its full range of experience. Even antiwar literature, despite its best intentions, often manages to convey the same idea. Some historians have taken the notion so far as to portray history as nothing more than a succession of wars and battles, as if all human progress depended exclusively on physical conflict, on epic showdowns, and on desperate struggles for survival. In these portrayals, war may showcase the worst that humans are capable of, yet it can also bring out the best—honor, bravery, self-sacrifice, camaraderie, glory, and the capacity for rising to a challenge. It can sweep across the landscape of broken lives and pluck a mediocre man out of obscurity, elevating him into a position of fateful importance. The experience of war can expose the frontline soldier to a rush of feelings and sensations so exotic and so visceral that they can never be equaled. Simply being there becomes the defining moment of his life. As for the poor reader, the vicarious experience of war bestows a sinking feeling of having missed out. Like so many other Walter Mittys, he can only wonder what he might have done had he been there.

Shakespeare undoubtedly had in mind the Walter Mitty in all of us when he composed the king's stirring prebattle speech at Agincourt in *Henry V*. In it he confirms the notion that every dire predicament presents the opportunity of a lifetime because it encompasses two extremes: glorious success or abject failure. This explains a pervasive theme of prebattle speeches—that we have only to imagine success for it to be ours. On the morning of the battle, the king gathers his men for one final blessing and tells them why they should consider themselves, outnumbered though they may be, lucky to be there:

> He that outlives this day and sees old age,
> Will yearly on the vigil feast his neighbors

And say, "Tomorrow is Saint Crispian."

Then will he strip his sleeve and show his scars,

And say, "These wounds I had on Crispin's day."

Old men forget; yet all shall be forgot,

But he'll remember, with advantages,

What feats he did that day. . . .

And Crispin Crispian shall ne'er go by,

From this day to the ending of the world,

But we in it shall be remembered.

Dulce et Decorum Est pro Patria Mori

One of the principal themes of war literature, going as far back as the Bible and the works of the Greek historians, is the honor of taking part and the shame of missing out. Some warriors handle it well; others do not. For example, when an Athenian army marched to Marathon to face down the Persian invaders in 490 BC, they called upon their Spartan allies to give aid. But they chose the wrong month. The Spartans were in the midst of celebrating a feast, and sent word that they could not march until the full moon. The battle took place on the very day the Spartans set off, and by the time they arrived at Marathon it was all over. The Athenian phalanx had destroyed the Persians in one of the most celebrated and (supposedly) lopsided battles in history. No one could have predicted it, and no one needed to tell the Spartans that they should have been there. They came anyway, they saw, they gave due praise to the victors, and marched home. The story as told by Herodotus stands as a monument to Spartan dignity if not as an object lesson, a reminder that not every dog gets to have his day (although ten years later, as we will see, the Spartans would indeed have their day in the sun).

Herodotus explores this theme elsewhere when he tells us of Callicrates, "the most beautiful man not only among the

Spartans but in the whole Greek camp," who died at the Battle of Plataea, but not *in* battle. While standing in the ranks waiting to march against the enemy, he was struck in the side by an arrow.

> While his comrades advanced to the fight, he was borne out of the ranks, very loath to die . . . "I grieve," said he, "not because I have to die for my country, but only because I have not lifted my arm against the enemy, or done any deed worthy of me, much as I have desired to achieve something."

The same fate would befall Charles Ardant du Picq. After being mortally wounded by a shell fragment as his unit marched to the field of battle at Longeville-les-Metz in August of 1870, he lamented that, "My regret is to be struck in this way, without having been able to lead my regiment on the enemy."

Many soldiers are killed before getting a chance to fight, yet we never distinguish them from those who died fighting. All who go off to battle win respect, but those who miss the battle entirely, as Herodotus makes clear, are disgraced. The Battle of Plataea in 479 BC, he tells us, provided a few examples.

> . . . the Mantineans arrived upon the field, and found that all was over, and that it was too late to take any part in the battle. Greatly distressed hereat, they declared themselves to deserve a fine, as laggards; after which, hearing that a portion of the Medes had fled away under Artabazus, they were anxious to go after them as far as Thessaly. The Lacedaemonians however would not suffer the pursuit; so they returned home to their own land, and sent the leaders of their army into banishment. Soon after the Mantineans, the Eleans likewise arrived, and showed the same sorrow; after which they too returned home, and banished their leaders.

Ten years after the Battle of Marathon (or one book of Herodotus' *History* later), the Spartans did get their chance to make up for not being at Marathon. Instead of a day in the sun, the event at Thermopylae turned out to be six days in the shadow of death. Herodotus himself invoked this imagery in his tale of the Spartan Dieneces, who was warned before the battle that, "Such was the number of the barbarians that when they shoot forth their arrows the sun would be darkened by their multitude." Dieneces welcomed the news as excellent tidings, and with the requisite élan added that "if the Medes darken the sun, we shall have our fight in the shade."

From such seeds did the renown of the Spartans flower into a cult. Almost every heroic defense thereafter would be likened to a Thermopylae, and conversely, the most ignoble acts of war would stand in stark contrast to the Spartans' remarkable dignity and self-control. Thucydides may well have had this in mind when he chose to relate an unfortunate incident from the Peloponnesian War about an army that had arrived too late, like the Spartans at Marathon, but did not handle it quite so nobly.

In 410 BC, seventy years after Thermopylae, the Athenians were at war with the Spartans. Pericles, their great and principled leader who had led them into the conflict twenty years earlier, was long since dead, and with him had died the noble rationale for the war. Now largely concerned with wealth and power, the Athenians were about to embark upon an ill-fated invasion of Sicily that seemed dubious from the start. No longer relying solely on a citizen's army, they had taken to hiring mercenaries from around the Mediterranean, among whom numbered the Dii, a nomadic and warlike Thracian tribe. Having set out for Athens with the requisite enthusiasm, the Dii had the misfortune to arrive too late. Not having extra funds to keep them in their pay, the Athenians sent them home, encouraging them to plunder off non-allied cities along the way. In their lust for some form of bloody compensation, the Thracians stormed the unexpecting and practically undefended city of Mycalessus, with predictably appalling results. According to Thucydides:

> The Thracians bursting into Mycalessus sacked the
> houses and temples, and butchered the inhabitants,

sparing neither youth nor age but killing all they fell in with, one after the other, children and women, and even beasts of burden, and whatever other living creatures they saw; the Thracian people, like the bloodiest of the barbarians, being ever most murderous when it has nothing to fear. Everywhere confusion reigned and death in all its shapes; and in particular they attacked a boys' school, the largest that there was in the place, into which the children had just gone, and massacred them all. In short, the disaster falling upon the whole city was unsurpassed in magnitude, and unapproached by any in suddenness and in horror.

Next to such indiscriminate despoilers the Spartans seem positively enlightened; but of course they were not. Their social structure, built as it was around the practice of warfare, had much to be deplored: the segregation of young boys who were brought up as warriors; the ritual practice of murder, in which young men got a taste for killing by practicing the art on slaves, criminals, outsiders, and the lower caste; and a negligible artistic or literary heritage. In short, Sparta systematized the appalling treatment of an underprivileged majority, and by doing so sustained an elite that was unconscionably brutal. And yet, for all that, at least they weren't the Dii. In war they handled themselves with honor and dignity, and they continue to inspire admiration as exemplars of military prowess, virtue, and above all, self-control on the battlefield. Much of that respect rests upon Thermopylae, the defining event of Spartan culture.

Go Tell the Spartans

The defense of Thermopylae in 480 BC has generated intense discussion not just about what happened, but about why. Herodotus provides us with the most detailed account of the incident, but its many gaps and inconsistencies tend to blur the motivations of those who fought to the death and those who

171

withdrew before the final action. Did Leonidas have to make a final stand? The consensus seems to be that, as a purely practical matter, he did not. A delaying action would have been adequate and, as Leonidas probably knew, quite feasible.

His task was to head off a large Persian army by confronting it at a narrow pass between the mountains and the sea. It was the most defensible position on the principal route into Greece from the north, a route that the invading Persians, confident in the overwhelming might of their large army, were sure that the Greeks could not contest. Many of the Greek city-states had already gone over to the Persian side, and others were prepared to. Thus, while the confederation of defiant states, led by Athens and Sparta, gathered their navies, which constituted their true military power, they sent Leonidas to Thermopylae to buy some time. He took with him a royal bodyguard of 300 Spartan hoplites, along with an unknown number of helots (attendants of a lower caste). They were supported by a thousand Thespians and an unwilling contingent of Thebans who were ready at any moment to go over to the enemy.

After three days of fending off the invaders with this coalition, Leonidas began to think he could hold the Persians at bay indefinitely, until he discovered that his valiant band had been betrayed and was about to be surrounded. A traitorous local guide had tipped off King Xerxes about a pass that would lead the Persians around to the Greeks' rear guard. Yet there was still time for Leonidas to dismiss all of those who wished to leave.

The Spartan king knew from the oracle's prediction that either Sparta would be overthrown by its invaders, or its king must die. Herodotus speculates that in light of their absence at Marathon, Leonidas wished to secure all of the glory for his Spartans. Like Achilles at Troy, who knew from his mother's prophecy that if he killed Hector he too would perish, he chose duty over life. Among his band of 300, only two seriously contemplated the option of leaving (a third was away on an embassy to Thessaly). The rest voted to stick it out, and thus staged the ultimate "you were not there" scenario.

The two who had permission to leave were the brothers Aristodemus and Eurytus, both of whom suffered from an eye disease that had rendered them practically blind. Eurytus elected to stay, and told his helot attendants to buckle on his armor and lead him into the thick of the fighting, where he was cut down. But Aristodemus chose to return to Sparta, where, once the news of the valiant stand had made the rounds, he was treated with contempt. Shunned for the next 12 months, the chastened Aristodemus, his eyesight somewhat restored, eagerly marched off to the final expulsion of the Persians at the great Battle of Plataea in 479. There he threw himself upon the enemy with utter abandon and killed many before being cut down. Yet he won no glory because in his zeal to redeem himself he had left the phalanx, and the Greeks valued nothing more than the infantryman who remained in the ranks. Of the other survivor, who had been away on an embassy, Herodotus merely says that "on his return to Sparta, he found himself in such disgrace that he hanged himself."

It is a familiar story. To take just one example, a British officer in Wellington's army, Lieutenant Colonel Lord Portarlington, made the unpardonable mistake of failing to get back to his regiment before they charged at Waterloo. He was forced to resign in shame. Although he later purchased a commission with another regiment, his fellow officers shunned him, and in keeping with such tales, Portarlington died penniless, a broken man.

Meanwhile, back at the pass, Leonidas and his 300 men, along with 700 Thespians, fought on for three more days and "defended themselves to the last, such as still had swords using them, and others resisting with their hands and teeth; till the barbarians, who in part had pulled down the wall and attacked them in front, in part had gone round and now encircled them upon every side, overwhelmed and buried the remnant left beneath a shower of missiles." According to Herodotus, the

Greeks killed 20,000 Persians in this struggle, a number so large that Xerxes ordered all but 1000 of them to be buried in trenches and hidden by foliage, so that sightseers who flocked to the site would not see how so few had killed so many. But no one was deceived. The Thespians raised a monument to their dead, and so did the Spartans. On theirs they inscribed these celebrated words contributed by the poet Simonides that sum up the rationale for being there:

> Go tell the Spartans, thou that passest by,
>
> That here obedient to their words we lie.

To serve, to do one's duty, to be willing to die, to be honored for doing so—this is the recipe for honor.

Follow Me, and Dethrone the Czar

Notwithstanding Thermopylae, one of the strongest incentives to fight is to have fought and survived: not simply to have been there, but to have stood up to the danger, risked life and limb (presumably for a noble cause), and lived to fight another day. Although this does not explain the causes of wars, it does help us to understand why it is not difficult to raise an army. In all but the bloodiest of ages, the most plague-stricken of eras, or the most oppressive of military regimes, there has generally been a surplus of what one writer has referred to as "underemployed warriors"—a willing segment of the population who are more likely to cause trouble if they are *not* allowed to fight. One of the principal motivations behind the Crusades, it should be remembered, was to give underemployed warriors something to do other than wreak havoc across Europe.

The urge to "be there" has inspired many to go off to war in search of meaning—to live, and possibly die, for a cause. This urge led George Orwell to enlist in the Red Brigades during the Spanish Civil War, an experience which he chronicled in his book *Homage to Catalonia*. In Stendahl's *The Charterhouse of Parma*, the young and dazzlingly naive Fabrizio sets out to fulfill his fantasy of serving Napoleon as a cavalry officer, only to arrive at the Battle of Waterloo (not having any idea what he has stumbled upon) in time to be unceremoniously mistreated by cheats, cutthroats, and scoundrels, many of whom happen to be officers and gentlemen. What he finds, of course, is the reality of war—a horrifying parody of the heroic tales that fill his head. Once he is welcomed into the company of some war-weary veterans—deserters, as it happens—there is nothing left to prove except a capacity for survival.

Karl von Clausewitz, the Prussian general considered by many to be the foremost analyst of war, noted that, "Of all the passions that inspire man in battle, none, we have to admit, is so powerful and so constant as the longing for honor and renown." He should have added the longing to be considered a man among the men with whom one fights. This, in fact, is an even more powerful motivator. Combat has always served as a rite of passage, a fact reflected in the vocabulary of war more than the practice of it. Soldiers are tested by fire or tempered by it. Once tested, the rank and file become a brotherhood. Commanders are father figures, but they also serve as priests who preside over the sacrifice in which the troops are bloodied. Blood, the symbol of ritual purification, is the red badge of courage invoked by Stephen Crane in the title of his master-work, a story that cannot be fully appreciated outside the context of the cult of fraternalism, a simulated rite of passage that swept the country in the wake of the Civil War.

In their unceasing quest for acceptance into the brother-hood, all men become fascinated, if not obsessed, by danger. This fascination attaches not only to danger in itself, but to men who routinely face it: men in dangerous jobs, men who explore unknown worlds, men who subject themselves to extreme conditions. The list includes steelworkers, fishermen, miners, mountaineers, Arctic explorers, and solo voyagers. But none of these can quite compete with the warrior, who at different times becomes all of these things. The contrast with the desk worker and the executive could not be more stark. The eighteenth-century scholar and critic Samuel Johnson knew this, and one day, while talking to his biographer Boswell about war, he shifted the conversation to the gulf between those who have been there and those who have not.

"Every man thinks meanly of himself for not having been a soldier, or not having been at sea," he said, prompting Boswell to note the exception of Lord Mansfield. "Sir," replied Johnson, "if Lord Mansfield were in a company of General Officers and Admirals who have been in service, he would shrink; he'd wish to creep under the table." When Boswell attempted to parry this thrust, Johnson went further. "No, Sir; were Socrates and Charles the Twelfth of Sweden both present in any company, and Socrates to say, 'Follow me, and hear a lecture on philosophy'; and Charles, laying his hand on his sword, to say, 'Follow me, and dethrone the Czar'; a man would be ashamed to follow Socrates. Sir, the impression is universal; yet it is quite strange." But not so strange that Johnson cannot explain it: "Sir, the profession of soldiers and sailors has the dignity of danger. Mankind reverence those who have got over fear, which is so general a weakness."

This explains, in a nutshell, why there has never been a shortage of young men willing to fight. One only has to say, "Come with me and dethrone the Czar," or, as Cyrus did, "Come with me and usurp my brother's throne and enjoy the riches of Persia," and one finds oneself with a cohort of 10,000 Greeks and assorted other mercenaries, revolutionaries, visionaries, and hooligans, ready to march off to the fight.

Ironically, Johnson, who should have known better, chose the wrong man as his foil. Socrates may have been a philosopher, but he had been to war and had served admirably. He had fought in the phalanx at Potidaea and Delium, and given the chance to go off to war again or listen to a lecture on philosophy, he would undoubtedly have chosen to do both. In Plato's *Symposium*, the Athenian general Alcibiades recalls serving with Socrates at Potidaea, where the philosopher not only displayed bravery, endurance, and a keen sense of duty, but also a tireless capacity to philosophize.

> One day, at dawn, he started thinking about some problem or other; he just stood outside, trying to figure it out. He couldn't resolve it, but he wouldn't give up. He simply stood there, glued to the same spot. . . . He was still there when evening came, and after dinner some Ionians moved their bedding outside, where it was cooler, . . . but mainly to watch if Socrates was going to stay out there all night. And so he did; he stood on the very same spot until dawn! He only left the next morning, when the sun came out, and he made his progress to the new day.

As for his behavior in battle, Socrates acquitted himself honorably in the retreat from Delium in 424 BC. The Athenians had encroached on the enemy's territory and, unable to hold it, were routed by the Boeotian army. Yet during the retreat Socrates acted the part of the pursuer more than the pursued. According to Alcibiades, "In the midst of the battle he was making his way exactly as he does around town—with swaggering gait and roving eye. . . . Even from a great distance it was obvious that this was a very brave man, who would put up a terrific fight if anyone approached him." Which pretty nicely summarizes his approach to philosophy.

Alcibiades himself was not afraid to follow Socrates, nor afraid to lead others into battle, however incautiously. A respected general, although not an entirely patriotic one, Alcibiades talked the Athenians into the disastrous Sicilian expedition. In the midst of it, being accused of treasonous acts, he went over to the Spartan side, and from there to the Persians, and finally back to the Athenians. His genius was not merely tactical but political, and his career only underlines Johnson's point that the profession of soldiers and sailors has the dignity of danger, and that we will forgive many things in those who in desperate times prove they can master fear, "which is so general a weakness." Many a

177

prebattle speech and many a politician's call to arms dwell on the very idea that time waits for no one, and that glory goes to the man who reaches for it. Those who do not act quickly enough, like the Dii, will simply miss the boat.

Where Wert Thou, Brave Crillon?

A final note on Louis Crillon. He lived 72 years, served bravely under two kings, fought in countless battles, and even commanded a galley at the Battle of Lepanto, serving under Don John of Austria in the last naval action involving oared galleys. One historian illustrates his passion for conflict with a charming anecdote in which the young Crillon, moved almost to tears by a sermon on the sufferings of Christ during Passion Week, jumped to his feet from his pew, drew his sword halfway, and reproached himself, crying out, "In Heaven's name, where wert thou, brave Crillon, in that hour?" Yet one instance of not being there may have saved his reputation. He was fortunate enough to have been away from Paris at the time of the infamous St. Bartholomew's Day massacre.

Henry IV's letter, which Voltaire misquotes, had nothing to do with Arques, a brilliant short-handed victory fought in 1593. The occasion of the letter was the siege of Amiens, which occurred later. Here is the text of the letter, written in Henry's characteristically buoyant style:

> Go hang yourself, brave Crillon, for not having been at my side on Monday last, on the fairest occasion man ever saw or ever perhaps will see again. Believe me that I wished you there. The cardinal came on in a fine fury, but only to return shamefully whence he came. I hope next Thursday to be within Amiens itself, where I remain only long enough to prepare a new enterprise, for I now have one of the finest armies you could conceive. It lacks for nothing but the brave Crillon, who will always be welcome to me and well regarded. Adieu.

But now my death is upon me.
Let me at least not die without a struggle, inglorious,
but do some big thing first, that men shall come to
know of it.

Hector to Achilles
At the walls of Troy
The *Iliad* of Homer, book XXII, line 303

It will surely be sweet, through some manly and
noble thing which one may say or do today, to keep
himself in remembrance among those whom he wishes
to remember him.

Xenophon
Anabasis

England expects that every man will do his duty.

Admiral Horatio Nelson
Battle of Trafalgar
21 October 1805

Damn the torpedoes! Four bells, Captain Drayton, go
ahead! Jouett, full speed!

Admiral David G. Farragut
Battle of Mobile Bay
5 August 1864

The Hartford *collides with the ironclad* Tennessee *at the Battle of Mobile Bay, August 5, 1864. Sketched by Frank H. Schell for* Battles and Leaders of the Civil War.

CHAPTER ELEVEN

Damn the Torpedoes!

FARRAGUT AT MOBILE BAY (1864)

England Expects

For more than a century a remarkable bronze likeness of David Farragut has graced a shady corner of New York City's Madison Square. Crafted by the eminent sculptor Augustus Saint-Gaudens, it succeeds like no sculpture of that era in capturing a man of action who fought the good fight. Although life-size, it qualifies as monumental. Yet in keeping with the American tradition, it also reveals a man who was merely doing a job and doing it well.

In his *History of Warfare*, the eminent military historian John Keegan notes that "war in art always calls forth from the artist the representation of the potential and the sensational, rather than of documentary realities." Well, perhaps not always. Saint-Gaudens's unique talent was his ability to bring out the potential rather than the sensational, while still being faithful to the documentary realities. He never succumbed to the fashion for portraying modern men as Greek gods, for example. Nevertheless, his heroes are larger than life. His Farragut, unlike Nelson at the top of his column in London's Trafalgar Square, is a great man, but recognizably one of us. His feet are planted firmly on the deck, which is not too far above the ground.

During his lifetime and after, David Farragut was frequently compared to Horatio Nelson, and not without reason. Nelson's place on his pedestal, like Farragut's, was won through a lifetime of service, and for better or worse would also come to be summed up by a single phrase, in Nelson's case a message he sent to his fleet prior to engaging the French off Cape Trafalgar in 1805. "England expects that every man will do his duty" is how the message came out, but not how he originally intended it. In his first attempt to come up with something suitably inspirational, the admiral wrote down this less-than-memorable sentiment: "Nelson confides that every man will do his duty." Sensing that the words fell short of the mark, one of his officers tactfully suggested that the commander might do well to replace his own name with that of the home-land. England, he thought, should fit into it somehow. Nelson agreed. "England confides that every man will do his duty" would be the order of the day. Yet something was still not quite right. The word *confides* seemed to lack the proper sense of urgency. What's more, it was not in the signal book.

In the first half of the nineteenth century, ships of the British navy communicated with flags using a system developed in the late 1700s by Sir Hugh Popham. Popham's book, *Telegraphic Signal, or Marine Vocabulary*, established the lexicon of words that could be communicated by this form of short-hand. Any word not in Popham's vocabulary had to be spelled out letter by letter. It was Nelson's flag lieutenant, John Pascoe, who pointed out to the admiral that the word *confides* was not contained in Popham's book, and thus would have to be spelled out. Knowing his lexicon inside and out, Pascoe suggested that the word *expects* might do just as well. The order was run up the flagpole, and a legend was born.

The lesson, it seems, is that every great general needs a good editor, or at least a good press agent. As the Nelson anecdote suggests, not every tactical genius has the gift of pith. Even when a commander's words do rise to the occasion, they often fall like the proverbial tree in the forest. If he is lucky, or if the gravity of the occasion demands it, some revisionist will come along to insert a few scenes, add voice-overs and a soundtrack, and amplify the story for effect. In Nelson's case, his crew contributed the rewrites and his biographer, the poet Robert Southey, turned his subject into a schoolboy's hero.

Ironically, Nelson's famous order was more enthusiastically received by posterity than by the fleet. Upon seeing it, Rear Admiral Cuthbert Collingwood, Nelson's second in command, impatiently remarked, "I wish Nelson would stop signaling, as we all know well enough what we have to do." This, of course, is not the stuff of legend, and Southey (who, by the way, also gave us Goldilocks and The Three Bears) naturally left it out of his account. Besides, Collingwood should have known the message was not for him. It was meant for the history books.

Then again, Nelson did not secure his reputation by always saying the right thing at the right time. He did it by putting his life on the line and winning important naval battles. He died at Trafalgar after being shot by a French sniper, but not before assuring himself that the battle was won. "Thank God I have done my duty," he is reputed to have muttered before expiring. Such a man did not need to court popularity or cater to the press. It mattered little that he was not well liked or that he made a poor impression on those who met him. One contemporary referred to him as a "complete booby." The Duke of Wellington, in his only encounter with Nelson, found him to be "so vain and so silly as to surprise and almost disgust me." But if Nelson on land was like Mozart away from his keyboard, he was as great a genius in his proper element—at sea—and what character flaws he may have possessed cannot deflate his reputation. He could sail, he could fight, his sailors loved and respected him, and most importantly, he won battles. Had he never uttered a single memorable phrase, history would have supplied the deficit.

Like Nelson, the Duke of Wellington is credited with a famous phrase, but in his case it is a complete fabrication, a put-up job that his followers have come to despise. The phrase "The Battle of Waterloo was won on the playing fields of Eton" is a good example of what one historian has called a "social misconstruction of reality." Wellington never said any such thing, and would have bristled at the assertion. He despised Eton. But the quote served to reinforce a petty conceit about the superiority of the English elite schools and their monopoly on character. It turns out that Eton did not have organized team sports in Wellington's day, and besides, the duke did not go in for sports. Nor did he believe that the officer corps had more to do with the outcome at Waterloo than the rank and file. He did believe that the day would have been lost had he not been there, but he gave Eton no credit for that. The quote surfaced three years after Wellington's death, went through a process of revision, and landed in the pages of unsubstantiated monumental history shortly thereafter. It tells us nothing about Wellington or his army, but quite a bit about the ease with which popular history can and does masquerade as legitimate history.

The Use and Abuse of History

The words attributed to Nelson and Wellington, while peripheral to military history, begin to suggest why the subject has come under fire. Military history has been criticized for imposing order where there was chaos, for breaking up the continuity of unfolding events into discrete episodes, and for spinning the facts in order to impart moral, political, or tactical lessons. Add to this a tendency to invent or insert unlikely or unreliable quotations, simplistic maxims, and blustery battle orders, and it would seem that military history is a hopelessly muddled enterprise.

Yet while it often veers toward the improbable and outrageous, history writ large is irresistible. The memoirs and maxims of Napoleon, Caesar, and Frederick the Great, for example, are full of invented scenes, imagined dialogue, relentless action, and impressive numbers that may disappoint us when we first see through them. Yet most of us never get that far. This is because the military historical tradition is dominated by writ-

184

ers whose allegiance has always been (and still is) to the requirements of a good story, and who don't want awkward facts (or the absence of facts) to interfere with the narrative.

As one scholar, commenting on the works of the celebrated fourteenth-century French chronicler Jean Froissart, noted, "we ought surely to respect and preserve the mystery of those passages which, if baldly 'demythified,' would lose much of their appeal and charm." Froissart was not technically a chronicler. A chronicle, properly speaking, is a spare chronology of events, whereas a history is more of a story. Froissart thought of his work as history more than chronicle, and in his attempt to impart moral lessons he naturally had to make things up. The result is entertaining: as the epic struggle between the Plantagenet and Valois clans unfolds in the pages of Froissart, the fate of Western Europe hangs in the balance. The narrative is so compelling that, in the absence of anything better, Froissart's *Chronicle* became the standard history of the Hundred Years' War, and served as the primary source for official histories up until the nineteenth century. It still provides quotes (invented ones) for unsuspecting historians who assume that history books never lie. Well-meaning historians, both amateur and professional, continue to swallow its outrageous tales and pass them along as fact. The trick is to be entertained while not getting caught taking such embellishments as the literal truth.

It helps to concede that there are different types of history that serve different purposes. In a small book whose English title is *The Use and Abuse of History*, the German philosopher Friedrich Nietzsche listed three things that history can, should, and does do: glorify greatness, preserve traditions, and pass judgment on past deeds. Seeing these as distinct categories, Nietzsche gave them names—monumental history, antiquarian history, and critical history—that provide us with a useful way of thinking about military history in particular. The reported deeds of Nelson, Wellington, and Farragut, for example, fall into the realm of the monumental, a type of history that is necessary to the man of action who fights the good fight and needs examples from great figures of the past, examples he cannot find among his contemporaries. At the other end of the spectrum, in the realm of critical history, we are led to dissect and debunk accounts of the past and the moral lessons they supposedly contain. In Nietzsche's words, "Man must have the strength to break up the past . . . bring the past to the bar of judgment, interrogate it remorselessly, and finally condemn it. Every past is worth condemning." Somewhere between idealizing the past and trampling on it lies the impulse to study it dispassionately, like a scientist analyzing the chemical composition of a great painting in order to decide how best to preserve it.

According to Nietzsche, all three ways of looking at history serve life, but an overemphasis on any one of them is harmful. Too close an examination of the past renders it useless. "A historical phenomenon," he wrote, "completely understood and reduced to an item of knowledge, is, in relation to the man who knows it, dead."

In the histories of battles, there is no danger of achieving complete understanding. War can never be reduced to an item of knowledge, and as a result will never die out. But if we can't completely understand it, we should at least understand the way we talk about it. Much of monumental history—Herodotus' numbers or Froissart's dialogue, for example—is fobbed off as antiquarian history. Colorful details that liven up a good story are frequently mistaken for facts. Moreover, much of what passes for critical history reinforces such mistakes by confusing monumental history with documentary truth. For example, King Harold is often criticized for attacking prematurely at the Battle of Hastings, before the rest of his army had arrived. The only problem with this critique is that the "rest of his army" didn't exist. The second-guessers base their judgment on a persistent rumor.

While characters like Nelson, Wellington, and Farragut are known primarily through monumental histories that portray them as upholders of the tradition of bold enterprise personified by Alexander the Great, they have also been subjected to other types of scrutiny. The antiquarians revel in the details of their battles: the uniforms, insignia, armaments, formations, and battle conditions. The critics point out the mistakes made, the defects of character, and the inglorious actions of some of the men. What is needed, and what is sorely lacking, is some balance. No one of these approaches, according to Nietzsche, should prevail over the others.

That point brings us back to David Farragut and what happened at Mobile Bay. It is a story that is almost always served up as monumental history, not through tampering with the facts but through selective emphasis. When it is not simply recapped in two sentences (as it often is), the story always gets the same spin: in the retelling, the battle hinges on a momentous decision made by a bold leader in the face of dire peril. Yet Farragut's own version of the event sounds nothing like this. Judging by the reports he filed, he was so wrapped up in the ultimate goal that he failed to appreciate his own dramatic role in a key juncture of American history. Then again, perhaps it is we who have it all wrong. Perhaps history (or posterity), dazzled as it was by those three words—"Damn the torpedoes"—missed the real story. What did happen at Mobile Bay? What happened afterward? Certainly Farragut, who was not entirely happy with his decisions that day, would have been dismayed that the most notable result of the day's action turned out to be a lasting contribution to the American language, and that the event itself, in less than a century, would fade almost completely from the nation's collective memory.

Farragut at Mobile Bay

After his exploits in seizing New Orleans and securing the Mississippi up to Vicksburg, David Farragut was promoted to the rank of admiral, the first American to earn that honor. Shortly thereafter, in quick succession, the Union took

Vicksburg, and Port Hudson also capitulated. Farragut's initial mission had been fulfilled, but he still had something to prove. He got the chance to do it late in 1863, when the Secretary of the Navy turned the command of the Mississippi over to Rear Admiral David Porter, and gave Farragut the task of capturing the remaining Confederate-held ports in the Gulf of Mexico.

Farragut got off to a rough start. Almost immediately he suffered two major setbacks when his far-flung command suffered the loss of the port of Galveston and the river channel at Sabine Pass. These successive embarrassments threatened to spoil Farragut's record. He had a chance to make amends, however, if he could capture the Union's final and most critical naval objective—the port of Mobile, Alabama. It was not going to be easy.

At the mouth of Mobile Bay, some thirty miles south of the port city, two Confederate forts, Morgan and Gaines, stood silent watch over the entrance to the bay. During the early months of 1864 Farragut painstakingly reconnoitered the approach, and what he saw looked dauntingly familiar. The enemy had driven a line of piles from Fort Gaines straight across to the navigable channel running close by Fort Morgan. In addition to the piles, they had laid a minefield in the channel itself, further restricting boat traffic to a lane that passed within a perilous 250 yards of the guns of the fort.

Farragut's fleet, for the moment not yet at full strength, had been blockading the outlet to the bay through the winter of 1863–64, at about the same time that Sherman was marching on Atlanta. For months Farragut had been waiting for some ironclads to bolster his firepower before taking on the forts. As for himself, now a man of 63, Farragut was no longer feeling particularly robust. The pressures of the Mississippi campaign had worn him down, and he suffered from either rheumatism or gout or both. As the blockade continued into the spring, the admiral's health recovered, but bad news continued to plague him. First the Union suffered a string of setbacks, including Lee's initial victory over Grant at Chancellorsville. Then

Farragut learned that the Confederates had succeeded in hauling the ironclad *Tennessee* from inland over a sandbar and into Mobile Bay. It spelled potential disaster for Farragut, whose wooden vessels could not contend with it.

The *Tennessee* was commanded by Admiral Franklin "Buck" Buchanan, who had made a name for himself at the helm of the ironclad *Merrimack* in its historic encounter with the *Monitor* at Hampton Roads in 1862. His new ship, which had been rushed into service, signaled the future of naval warfare. Built in the style of the *Merrimack*, it was arguably the most powerful warship in the world. At 209 feet in length and clad in three layers of two-inch thick iron plate, it would prove to be impervious to solid shot, immune from ramming, and more than a match for any wooden ship. Yet it was not invincible.

Farragut, a wooden ship man to the core, had good reasons to fear the *Tennessee*, and yet, like all the captains in his fleet, he refused to acknowledge its superiority and made it his prime objective. By July he had settled on his plan of attack: he would lead his fleet through the channel and past the guns of Fort Morgan with his wooden ships tied two abreast. The ironclad monitors (which had finally arrived) would run in single file alongside. Leading the column of monitors would be the *Tecumseh*, commanded by Captain T.A.M. Craven. Leading the main column of tethered ships would be the *Brooklyn*, sister ship to Farragut's *Hartford*, commanded by Captain James Alden. Following close behind would be the flagship itself, captained by Percival Drayton and tethered to the side-wheeler *Metacomet*, under Captain James E. Jouett. Ten more warships would follow in similar fashion.

After months of preparation and waiting, the moment finally arrived for Farragut to get under way. On the morning of August 5, the fleet weighed anchor, formed up in two columns, and proceeded to the entrance of Mobile Bay. The gunners in the fort were ready; the Confederate fleet, led by the *Tennessee*, stood at general quarters just above the fort. The Union column, with the monitor *Tecumseh* in the vanguard, entered the channel. Captain Craven initiated the proceedings by firing twice upon the fort, and soon the thunder of shell and shot, the clouds of smoke, and the flash of gun muzzles filled the channel. The all-too-familiar spectacle had begun once again.

At first the plan proceeded as expected. As each pair of tethered ships came within range and began firing on the fort, Confederate gunners fired back. At the same time the small Confederate fleet, led by the formidable *Tennessee*, moved to the head of the channel in order to intercept Farragut's monitors. This time, however, unlike at New Orleans, Farragut almost immediately faced a catastrophe.

Craven, piloting the *Tecumseh*, ceased all firing after his two initial shots in order to concentrate on the *Tennessee*. Quite possibly he had in mind a reenactment of the showdown between the *Monitor* and the *Merrimack*. He had been told to go to the right of a buoy that was thought to mark the end of the minefield. But seeing just how far to the right it lay, and wary that the Confederate ships might try to flee, Craven instead headed to the left of the buoy, and into the minefield. The other monitors followed, forging a path that cut off the main column. Alden, in the steam frigate *Brooklyn*, immediately cut his engine, then began backing his ship, and signaled the *Hartford* for instructions—in army code.

Several army signalmen had been brought aboard the *Hartford* and the *Brooklyn* to communicate with the ground troops sent to support the naval action. Farragut had ordered his army signalers belowdecks. They were too important to risk losing during the passage, and besides, the flag officer had ordered the fleet to use navy signals. But at this crucial juncture, with the stalled fleet coming under heavy fire, a furious Farragut was forced to summon Army Lieutenant John Coddington Kinney and send him up the foremast to read the signals and respond. Kinney had never before been 100 feet above the deck of a ship. Needless to say, he had never been quite so exposed to an artillery barrage either.

Captain Alden, it turned out, had merely signaled to ask what he should do about the monitors in his path. Farragut sent back a signal to go ahead, but Alden hesitated, and the *Hartford's* pilot was forced to cut the flagship's engines. The entire column ground to a potentially disastrous halt. The shore batteries kept up their fire and began to inflict some appalling casualties among the men on deck. At the same time, the Confederate fleet was closing in.

As at New Orleans, smoke had enveloped the scene almost as soon as the firing commenced. Not only did the signalman on the *Hartford* take to the mast, but so did the ship's pilot, along with Farragut himself, as was his habit. When Farragut climbed into the port main rigging to get a better view, the prospect of seeing him fall onto the deck or overboard prompted Captain Drayton to send the quartermaster aloft to secure Farragut to the rigging. After putting up a small fuss, Farragut relented, and from that vantage, well within shouting distance of the pilot above and Captain Drayton below, he watched the drama unfold and the crisis develop.

Captain Craven, oblivious to the fact that he had brought both columns to a halt beneath the artillery barrage from Fort Morgan, had eyes only for the *Tennessee*, which he was hoping to take single-handedly. But when he got within a hundred yards of his goal, the crisis was reached: his monitor struck a torpedo at the easternmost extent of the minefield. In describing the explosion, some writers go so far as to say that the *Tecumseh* was literally blown out of the water, an obvious exaggeration, but it may well have seemed that way to witnesses. The ship's nose plunged instantly, causing its stern to rise out of the water, and the spectacle of the futile whirl of its screw left a lasting impression on all who saw it. The ironclad sank in less than two minutes. As Craven and his pilot, John Collins, rushed from the pilothouse to a hatchway so narrow that only one of them could pass, the captain gallantly yielded to the pilot, and Collins escaped. Craven went down with the ship, as did 93 men out of his crew of 114. Even General Page, the commander of the batteries on Fort Morgan, was appalled, and ordered his men not to fire on a boat sent by Farragut to try to rescue the drowning men.

With the entire Union column now stalled, the fleet slackened its fire. Captain Alden cast off his consort ship and again signaled for instructions. The entire fleet was now under heavy fire from the shore batteries. Farragut signaled Alden to move ahead, and again Alden hesitated. The *Brooklyn* blocked the way for the rest of the column, and the only way around it led directly through the minefield. As his biographers cannot resist saying, Farragut now faced the most momentous decision of his life.

When asked about it later, Farragut recalled that he uttered a prayer, and heard a voice that said to him, "Go on!" The submerged torpedoes lay in his path, but he had to take the chance that most of them had been laid so long ago that by now they would have leaked and been rendered harmless. The fate of the *Tecumseh* indicated otherwise, but Farragut chose to go ahead anyway, and he ordered the *Hartford's* pilot to take the lead. Alden, on board the stalled *Brooklyn*, is said to have shouted out that there was a heavy line of torpedoes across the channel, whereupon Farragut allegedly uttered the remark that secured his fame. "Damn the torpedoes," he supposedly shouted to Alden. Then to Captain Drayton: "Four bells, Captain Drayton, go ahead," and to Captain Jouett of the *Metacomet* he commanded, "Jouett, full speed!" As the *Hartford* passed over the buoys, the dull thudding of the torpedo cases and the snapping of fuses could be heard, but none exploded. The column proceeded into Mobile Bay to face off against the *Tennessee*.

The Main Event

The reports filed by the participants in the action at Mobile Bay run to about 250 pages. Despite the expected bureaucratic formality of tone and content, they do convey a sense of the momentousness of the battle. What they do not suggest is that Farragut at any time faced a critical moment of decision, that there was ever any option other than the one he chose, or that the key to the battle hinged upon actions or words that have since been immortalized. The words "Damn the torpedoes," in fact, are never mentioned.

The flag officer did lead the *Hartford* through the minefield, but the ship's captain, Percival Drayton, did not think this was worth noting in his summary. Farragut himself, in a report written at the end of the day, disposed of it in a sentence: "As we steamed up the Main Ship Channel there was some difficulty ahead and the *Hartford* passed on ahead of the *Brooklyn*." The *Hartford's* lieutenant commander, L. A. Kimberly, merely noted: "The *Brooklyn* now having stopped and commenced backing, the *Hartford* went ahead and led the fleet until we anchored up the bay." Captain Jouett of the *Metacomet* could add little more: "The *Brooklyn* backed down the line, when the *Hartford* shot ahead, leading the fleet past the forts." Captain Alden of the *Brooklyn*, perhaps sensing that he did not perform as splendidly as he might have, filed the most florid account, but he too passed over what we assume to be the dramatic high point with little more than a tip of the cap:

> We were now somewhat inside of the fort, when shoal water was reported, and at the same time as the smoke cleared up a little, a row of suspicious-looking buoys was discovered directly under our bows. While we were in the act of clearing them our gallant admiral passed us and took the lead.

"Damn the torpedoes" did not appear in any accounts of the battle until fourteen years after the event and eight years after Farragut's death. The words first show up in Foxhall Parker's *Battle of Mobile Bay* (1878), which draws almost every detail except the dialogue from the official records. There isn't much dialogue, but it is memorable. A year later Farragut's son Loyall picked up the phrase and included it in his biography of his father. From there it was off and running. Lieutenant Kinney, the army signalman, acknowledged the words in his gripping account of the battle reprinted in *Battles and Leaders of the Civil War*, but added that "there was never a moment when the din of battle would not have drowned out any attempt at conversation between the two ships."

At least one navy man has cast similar doubts on the story, noting that the noise of the artillery bombardment and the general confusion would have made any intelligible conversation between ships impossible. Nor would anyone aboard a ship under fire either have noticed or been able to hear the dull thudding of the mine cases or the snapping of their safety pins. Yet in his later years, after the phrase had become a figure of speech, Thom Williamson, the *Hartford's* chief engineer, would insist that Farragut gave him an order to "Go ahead," to which Williamson replied, "Shall I ring four bells, sir?" (Signals were conveyed to the engine room by bells; four bells meant to go forward as fast as possible.) Farragut responded, "Four bells—eight bells—sixteen bells—damn it, I don't care how many bells you ring!" Lieutenant John C. Watson confirmed the same story, also well after the event, and well after the phrase in question had become a legend. "I was standing on the poop deck at the time," he recalled, "and heard the admiral shout, on the instant, it seemed: 'Damn the torpedoes! Full speed ahead, Drayton! Hard a starboard! Ring four bells! Eight bells! Sixteen bells!' I think he also called to Commander Jouett of the *Metacomet* to back, for she did so." The order to Jouett makes sense because the *Hartford* had to make a hard left to get around the *Brooklyn*, which could only be done by spinning the tethered pair of ships—one in reverse, the other churning forward.

What is the truth of the matter? Even Farragut could not recall his exact words. What he does make clear is that the moment of decision should never have occurred, that he was embarrassed to have found himself having to go around the

Brooklyn at all. After a week had passed, allowing him time to compose his thoughts, he filed these comments on the incident:

> It was only at the urgent request of the captains and commanding officers that I yielded to the *Brooklyn* being the leading ship of the line, as she had four chase guns and an ingenious device for picking up torpedoes, and because, in their judgment, the flagship ought not to be too much exposed. This I believe to be an error, for apart from the fact that exposure is one of the penalties of rank in the Navy, it will always be the aim of the enemy to destroy the flagship, and . . . such attempt was very persistently made, but Providence did not permit it to be successful.

Here at last Providence gets due credit, for had Farragut been shot from the rigging, or had the *Hartford* been sunk by a mine, we would be unable to say "Damn the torpedoes" without a good deal of irony. But to speculate this way is to succumb to the "what if" syndrome that plagues history writing. In war, as in life generally, it is hard enough to know what did happen, much less what might have happened.

What did happen after the *Hartford* made it through the minefield, we tend to forget, was the real main event—the long-awaited showdown with the *Tennessee*. Running the channel was merely a prelude. The *Hartford* proceeded into the bay and was raked by fire from the Confederate gunboat *Selma*, a small side-wheeler that managed to inflict more damage with its four guns than all of the firepower of Fort Morgan. Buchanan also set off after the flagship in the *Tennessee*, as the rest of the Union fleet sat stalled before the minefield. But quite inexplicably, the *Tennessee* turned back after a brief pursuit, effectively deserting the overmatched *Selma*. The side-wheeler *Metacomet* was still lashed to the *Hartford*, and Captain Jouett pleaded with Farragut for the chance to go on the attack. When the flag officer at last gave in to the request, the

195

cables were cut and the *Metacomet*, easily the fastest ship in the bay, chased down the smaller ship and forced a surrender.

During this time, the remainder of the fleet had straightened itself out. The artillery barrage from the ships had momentarily silenced most of the guns of the fort, buying valuable time. As the *Brooklyn* led the way into the main ship channel, Buchanan's *Tennessee* appeared and bore down on the fleet. But again the Confederate commander seemed unable to single out an objective. Individually, any one of the wooden ships would have been helpless against him. Yet after some light action and a few attempted rammings, the encounter came to nothing. The fleet proceeded into the bay and regrouped with the *Hartford* about five miles above Fort Morgan.

The action, it seemed, was momentarily at an end, and the crews began to assess the damage. The swabbers, the surgeons, and the cooks set about their tasks, the latter laying out a well-deserved breakfast for the crew of the *Hartford*. But there would be no time to enjoy it. In an instant the call went up that the ram was coming, and the dishes were swept away. Buchanan had at last made a decision.

In history's last major action involving wooden ships, Farragut's steam frigates, side-wheelers, and monitors bore down on the Confederate ironclad. Hemmed in at every turn, the *Tennessee* kept firing, but the ship's weaknesses soon became apparent. Having been rushed too soon into battle, it had not been outfitted with an adequate engine. Making do with one from a smaller vessel, it was seriously underpowered. Still, the Union fleet could neither sink nor silence the *Tennessee* until they discovered its Achilles heel—her designers had left the rudder chains exposed. Once these were shot away, the ship's guns could no longer be brought to bear, and Buchanan, who had ceded command of the ship after sustaining a shrapnel wound that would cost him his leg, stoically gave permission for the raising of a white flag. With the loss of the *Tennessee*, the last hope for Mobile Bay vanished. The battle was over.

It Is Well That War Is So Terrible

With the passage of time critical events like the Battle of Mobile Bay quickly fade from memory. The world moves on. The news that kept us on the edge of our seats yesterday is, as we now say, history. It's gone. There are reminders, like Farragut's statue in Madison Square, to tell us that something important once happened, but such reminders tend to gloss over the unpleasant details, and the lessons are frequently lost over time.

The problem for military history is potentially serious. When war is rendered as an adventure story, it can lead to a collective yearning for something that never was. Leo Tolstoy had it right. He understood that we continue to get sucked into the romance of war, and into war itself, by forgetting what war is really like. At Fredericksburg, Robert E. Lee remarked to General James Longstreet, "It is well that war is so terrible, or we should grow too fond of it." Yet he had not counted on historians who forget to tell us how terrible, how senseless, how random, and ultimately how relentlessly human war really is.

Every people, every nation, and every generation have been conditioned to see war as a much more orderly, rational, and clear-cut business than it could possibly be, involving as it does real human beings. This is because the human element is usually suppressed in war narratives. In the interests of a good story, in the interests of morale, in the interests of sustaining the memory and good repute of those who sacrificed life and limb in the service of their country or their cause, historians necessarily maintain an illusion, one that is not limited to military matters. We encounter it in all walks of life. On the whole, we like to think that people perform the tasks entrusted to them better than they really do. It is the illusion of competence.

S.L.A. Marshall shattered this illusion when he pointed out the low rates of fire among World War II infantrymen, and when he suggested that the bulk of the work was done by a small core group of natural fighters. He was perceptive enough to draw a parallel to the workplace, where a minority does the real work. This seems plausible enough when applied to work, but we are less comfortable conceding the same fact in the realm of war. Yet even war is a job, and unlike almost any other sphere of human activity, it is something that cannot be rehearsed. No amount of training can approximate the experience of battle. Consequently, most soldiers are not prepared for it, and turn out to be not all that good at it—at least not as good as we are typically led to believe. War memoirs, the more candid ones anyway, concede that for all the pomp and ceremony that troops can demonstrate on the parade ground, once in battle, any semblance of order disappears. No matter how prepared they are, soldiers can only do what is humanly possible. As Helmuth von Moltke once observed, "No plan survives contact with the enemy."

Robert E. Lee had the premise right and the conclusion wrong. War is terrible, but with the passage of time we become fond of it in a nostalgic sort of way. War, it seems, is an inevitable side effect of human interaction, and while the past holds up many examples of its futility, horror, and madness, we tend to look the other way. In our reluctance to recall what happened or what price was paid, we are all too ready to forge ahead into the next conflict, and to say "Damn the torpedoes," which, in our ignorance of what the torpedoes were or what it means to damn them, has come to mean "Full speed ahead!" The irony, regrettably, is that this phrase has in effect become, among all the fighting words on record, the quintessential call to arms.

Farragut's flagship the Hartford. *Engraved by J. O. Davidson from a photo by J. W. Black for* Battles and Leaders of the Civil War.

Further Reading

In place of an exhaustive list of everything I read or consulted while researching this book, I decided to limit myself in this space to a list of works that I found to be particularly valuable in showing what happens in battle. These works constitute, in my opinion, a small but useful reference library for the reader who wishes to understand not just war, but the way war is portrayed in history.

Two short books that deserve more attention than they get (although they do not lack for it here) are Charles Ardant du Picq's *Battle Studies* and S.L.A. Marshall's *Men Against Fire*. Marshall, it should be noted, has himself come under fire for his methodology and some of the conclusions he reached in his studies of the Korean and Vietnam wars. Yet his book on World War II has stood the test of time, and it represents his best work. Another essential volume, one that set a standard for all subsequent war writers, is John Keegan's *The Face of Battle* (1978). Keegan begins with an insightful essay on the limitations of traditional drum-and-trumpet history writing, and follows up with a close look at the battles of Agincourt, Waterloo, and the Somme, showing how military history can and should be done. Those who are particularly drawn to Keegan's style and method might also wish to delve into his lengthier *History of Warfare* (1993).

Two other books worth reading focus on specific eras, but manage to illuminate the practice of war in all ages. They are Victor Davis Hanson's *The Western Way of War: Infantry Battle in Classical Greece* (1989) and Paddy Griffith's *Battle Tactics of the Civil War* (1989), both of which successfully debunk several persistent misconceptions.

I also recommend the opening chapter of the first volume of Hans Delbrück's *History of the Art of War*, in which he addresses the issue of army strengths. Perhaps more accessible (although harder to find) is his lecture dealing with popular misconceptions in military history, entitled *Numbers in History* (1913).

Leo Tolstoy's second epilogue to *War and Peace* contains an interesting essay on the limitations of history as told by historians versus artists (such as himself). It should, I hope, entice those who have not yet attempted it to read the entire novel, in which Tolstoy probes the causes and consequences of war in depth. Richard Hamilton's *The Social Misconstruction of Reality* (1996) is also worth a look, if only for its introduction and opening chapter on Wellington's alleged remark about Waterloo and Eton.

Thucydides' *History of the Peloponnesian War* is one of those rare works (like *War and Peace*) that seems to transcend its time, place, and subject by getting at the essence of human behavior in war and peace. I particularly recommend Robert Strassler's 1996 Free Press edition of the Crawley translation, which provides excellent maps, notes, and appendices. Xenophon's *Anabasis*, while less encyclopedic in scope, is also a good read.

Among modern memoirs, Robert Graves's *Good-Bye to All That* and George Orwell's *Homage to Catalonia* are fine examples of the kind of historical truth available, in Tolstoy's view, only to the artist.

Finally, Michael Howard's "The Use and Abuse of Military History" is an illuminating assessment of the difficulty of writing and reading military history. It can be found in Howard's *The Causes of War and Other Essays* (1983).

I also wish to acknowledge a few specific books that struck me as useful and dependable, and that helped me to shape my accounts of specific battles. Listed with the battles in question, they are:

The Battles of New Orleans and Mobile Bay:

   Charles Lee Lewis, *David Glasgow Farragut*, volume 2 (1941–43)

The Battle of Balaclava:

   Albert Seaton, *The Crimean War: A Russian Chronicle* (1977)

Sergeant York and the Argonne Offensive:

   David D. Lee, *Sergeant York: An American Hero* (1985)

Little Round Top:

   Mark Perry, *Conceived in Liberty: Joshua Chamberlain, William Oates, and the American Civil War* (1997)

The Siege of Bastogne:

   John S.D. Eisenhower, *The Bitter Woods* (1969)

   Trevor N. DuPuy, *Hitler's Last Gamble* (1995)

The Battle of Flamborough Head:

   Samuel Eliot Morison, *John Paul Jones: A Sailor's Biography* (1959)

   Augustus C. Buell, *Paul Jones, Founder of the American Navy* (1906)

The Siege of Fort William Henry:

   Francis Parkman, *Montcalm and Wolfe* (1884)

   Ian Kenneth Steele, *Betrayals: Fort William Henry and the Massacre* (1990)

Index

Delium, retreat from (424 BC), Socrates at, 177
Demaratus (exiled Spartan king), 136
Deuteronomy
    dismissal of unreliable fighters in, 115
    laws regarding sieges, 152-53
Devereaux, James, deputy U.S. commander at Wake Island, 141
Dictionary of Battles (Eggenberger), 123
Dictionary of Battles (Harbottle), 123
Dieneces, at Thermopylae, 170
Dii, sack of Mycalessus, 170-71
"Don't fire until you see the whites of their eyes!" xii
"Don't give up the ship!" 3
Drayton, Percival, 189, 191-93
Dubcek, Alexander, capitulation to the Soviets in 1968, 143

Ebb and Flow of Battle, The (Campbell), 76
Edward, the Black Prince, at Poitiers (1356), 110
Edward III, King of England, 160
"effectives," 111
Eisenhower, Dwight D., launching D-Day invasion, ix
Eisenhower, John, 145
El Cid, 47
"England expects . . . ," xi, 182-83
Epameinondas, at Leuctra (371 BC), 45

Ericsson, John, 16
Essling (1809), Napoleon at, 14
Eurytus, at Thermopylae, 173
"Every man for himself!" 90

Fair Maid of Perth (Scott), 116
Farragut, David Glasgow, U.S. admiral, 181, 186
    compared to Nelson, 14-15, 181
    at Mobile Bay, 4, 17-18, 187-96
    at New Orleans (1862), 6-13, 104
    reprimands Schley at Port Hudson, 15-16
    See also "Damn the torpedoes!"
Farragut, Loyall, biography of his father, 193
Farragut Memorial (New York), 181, 197
"fastest with the mostest," 71
Fifteen Decisive Battles of the World (Creasy), 119, 153
15th Alabama, 122
    at Little Round Top, 75, 79-81
"Fire at will!" xii, 47, 53, 67
fire on command, 67
Flamborough Head, Battle of (1779), 138-40, 142
Foch, Ferdinand, 49
Folts, Jonathan, 7
Fontenoy, Battle of (1745), 59-64, 67, 70
Foote, Shelby, 75
Forrest, Nathan Bedford, personal philosophy, 71

210

215

Two Moon, Chief, at Little Big
Horn, 69

Use and Abuse of History, The
(Nietzsche), 185

Valette, Jean de la, Siege of
Malta (1565), ix
Varnum, Charles A., at Little
Big Horn, 69
Vicksburg, Battle of (1863), 68,
187
Vollmer, German lieutenant,
Argonne offensive, 50-51
Voltaire, 134
on the Battle of Fontenoy,
59, 60, 62
Henriade, letter to Crillon,
165
misquoting Henry IV, 178

Wake Island, 141-43, 144
War and Peace (Tolstoy), 84
Bagration at Schön
Grabern, 101
War in the Middle Ages
(Contamine), 46
Waterloo, Battle of (1815), xi,
29, 112, 132-33
described by Stendahl, 175
Wellington quote, 183-84
Welles, Gideon
assigns Farragut to New
Orleans, 4

reassigns Farragut to the
Gulf, 188
Wellington, Arthur Wellesley,
Duke of, 186
fabricated quote on
Waterloo, 183-84
opinion of Nelson, 183
at Waterloo, xi, 112
West, Benjamin, 66
Westmoreland, Earl of, at
Agincourt, 115
Whittlesey, Charles, 49
Wilderness, Battle of the
(1864), 77
Williamson, Thom, 194
William of Poitiers, 93
William the Conqueror, at the
Battle of Hastings, 93
Wolfe, James, at Quebec, 64-66
Wolseley (assistant surgeon),
order to charge at
Inkermann (1854), 83

Xenophon, 102
on Cyrus the Great, 23
as historian, 98
prebattle speeches, 109
and the Ten Thousand, 98-
101
Xerxes, Persian emperor, at
Thermopylae, 120, 136-
37, 144, 172-74

York, Alvin, 47-53, 57, 58
comparison to Daniel
Boone, 52

About the Author

Brian Burrell is also the author of *The Words We Live By: The Creeds, Mottoes, and Pledges That Have Shaped America.* Both author and book have been prominently featured on The Today Show, on CNN's Booknotes, and in *USA Today, The Boston Globe,* and *Parade.*